SHERLOCK HOLMES: THE WAY OF ALL FLESH

Sherlock Holmes is called in to investigate when the body of an Italian diplomat is discovered in the River Thames, his torso horrifically mutilated. Fearing the political reper-cussions — the diplomat being in London to initiate talks regarding a secret naval treaty between the two nations — the Government entrust Holmes with the delicate task of uncovering the truth behind the brutal murder. Events take a shock-ing turn, however, when a young solicitor is found slain in the East End, his body similarly mutilated . . .

DANIEL WARD

---◆---

SHERLOCK HOLMES: THE WAY OF ALL FLESH

Complete and Unabridged

LINFORD
Leicester

First published in Great Britain

First Linford Edition
published 2005

British Library CIP Data

Ward, Daniel
  Sherlock Holmes: the way of all flesh.—
  Large print ed.—
  Linford mystery library
  1. Holmes, Sherlock (Fictitious character)—
  Fiction 2. Watson, John H. (Fictitious character)
  —Fiction 3. Detective and mystery stories
  4. Large type books
  I. Title
  823.9'2 [F]

  ISBN 1–84395–939–9

Published by
F. A. Thorpe (Publishing)
Anstey, Leicestershire

Set by Words & Graphics Ltd.
Anstey, Leicestershire
Printed and bound in Great Britain by
T. J. International Ltd., Padstow, Cornwall

This book is printed on acid-free paper

1

'MURDER!'

Is there any other word in the English language that can induce such a powerful response in all humans than that which echoed around the small sitting room of 221b Baker Street early in the morning of February 18th 1886. I had risen just before seven and, like most mornings, prepared to breakfast alone, my esteemed friend Sherlock Holmes never usually putting in his first appearance of the day until lunchtime at the earliest, before setting off for the surgery in Clerkenwell.

I had accepted an offer from an old medical colleague, with whom I had once studied at Barts, to take over his practice for two weeks while he and his family enjoyed a much-needed holiday in the Peak country. In truth, I had not been an active member of the profession since my demobilisation from the Army some five and a half years previously but the thought of an extra few pounds in my pocket to supplement the meagre pension the Government afforded me, not to mention the challenge of proving I still possessed the necessary skills for the job, convinced me to accept the offer. I very swiftly came to realise just why my friend had needed a break. Three days into my locum duties and I was drained, both physically and mentally. The practice had a large patient list and was known throughout London for the welcome it offered to all those who required treatment, regardless of social position or ability to pay. My friend, of good Christian stock, believed he had a moral duty to serve those less well off than himself, a noble sentiment indeed but one he was only able to put into practice after obtaining finance from several wealthy local sponsors.

I started my first day in the job with a genuine sense of goodness in my heart, so much so that I dispensed with the notion of taking a cab and walked the two miles from Baker Street to the surgery, which was located on the second floor of a converted warehouse in Chadwell Street. I arrived at the surgery at eight-thirty sharp, black leather medical bag clutched proudly in my right hand and my Member of the Royal College of Surgeons certificate in my inside breast-pocket, a necessity for all doctors in general practice and something I had brought along with me in the event that any of the patients, all of whom were strangers to me and I likewise to them, wanted proof of my testimonials before trusting me with their personal complaints. I was greeted by the extraordinary sight of a queue of people stretching as far as the next street. Initially, and somewhat naively, I believed they were queuing for some other purpose, casual labour perhaps in the other warehouses that lined the road, and was dismayed to discover they were all there for my personal attention.

It was almost nine o' clock in the evening when I forced myself to close the surgery doors on that first day, despite there still being some thirty or so patients, many coughing and spluttering terribly and others showing signs of a variety of ailments, patiently lining the corridor. I had never served as a general practitioner, despite possessing the qualifications and certificates to do so, but believed my experience as an army surgeon, performing life-saving treatment in the heat of battle while the roar of cannon-fire reverberated through the head like thunder, would stand me in good stead for anything the life of a London GP could throw at me. I was wrong. After three days, leaving the house just after seven each morning and not returning to almost ten at night, I felt in dire need of a holiday myself. Could locums employ locums, I, only half-jokingly, asked myself?

'You're clearly not as fit as you used to be,' Sherlock Holmes commented, taking his seat at the breakfast table before even I.

'I am thirty-five years old, Holmes,' was my somewhat tetchy reply. 'You make it sound as though I practically have one foot in the grave!'

'The way you walked in last night,

anybody would be forgiven for thinking so. There are only seventeen steps leading from the hall to this floor yet I noted you stopped twice to catch your breath.'

'I was very tired, that's why,' I explained. 'I worked my fingers almost to the bone yesterday. Almost fourteen hours with barely a break! I haven't a clue how Templeton does it, no wonder the man needs a holiday.'

'Dispensing care to the needy is his vocation,' said Holmes, slicing the top off his boiled egg with one fell swoop. 'For you it is a job of work and nothing more. I fear you will never make a general practitioner, Watson.* Perhaps you would be better suited finding yourself a handful of wealthy private patients to keep your bank balance healthy and your physical wellbeing even more so.'

'Chance would be a fine thing,' I replied. 'Anyway, right at this very moment in time, I am more interested in knowing what has caused Sherlock Holmes to rise from his pit at such an ungodly hour. When I turned in last night, you were still wide awake.' A thought, and not a very pleasant one at that, suddenly struck me. 'Don't tell me you haven't been to bed all night?'

I glanced over to Holmes's bureau, half-expecting, and secretly fearing, to see a hypodermic needle and bottle of cocaine solution on the desktop. I knew of only two things that kept Holmes awake all night, the intellectual stimuli provided by an investigation and the nervous energy provided by more artificial means, and I knew for a fact he was not employed on a case at present, a state of affairs he had been bemoaning only the day before. Holmes had read my thoughts and quickly sought to dismiss them.

'I have not taken recourse to the cocaine bottle,' he said firmly. 'I sleep when I am physically exhausted or bored out of my mind. Last night, I was neither.'

'A case?'

'Nothing quite so interesting, I am very much afraid to say. Just a small challenge I had set myself to read and memorise the entire contents of yesterday evening's *Pall Mall Gazette*.'

Holmes produced the said newspaper

and handed it to me across the table. 'Choose a sentence, my dear fellow. Any sentence.'

I opened the newspaper and glanced through the articles; the usual variety of city news, political and financial reports, social events, private agony columns and the day's racing results. I hadn't even seen a paper since taking over at the surgery and was looking forward to catching up on the news, albeit yesterdays. First things first, however, and I began to search for a suitable article to challenge Holmes. An item entitled 'OULTON TIPPED FOR NEWMARKET' attracted my attention and, as instructed, picked a sentence at random.

'The weather is tipped to be inclement for the time of year and this may favour . . . '

'Page eighteen, column two,' interrupted Holmes.

I frowned and tossed the paper onto the nearby armchair, intending to take it with me to read in the cab on the way to Clerkenwell. Even thinking about walking such a distance in my present condition brought blisters out on my feet.

'It would no doubt make an interesting parlour game but would such a skill have any merit in the real world?'

'Negligible,' Holmes admitted and, with a flick of the wrist, threw his spoon across the table in disgust. 'These eggs are hard again. Mrs. Hudson!'

I smiled to myself, taking care not to allow Holmes to be aware of my amusement, and theatrically produced a spoonful of golden-yellow yolk, perfectly runny and cooked to a tee, from the egg on my plate.

'Mrs. Hudson clearly removed your eggs from the pan first,' my friend said in a distinct huff. 'By the time they were so decoratively arranged upon your tray and the good lady returned to collect mine, they had been simmering for at least another three quarters of a minute. She keeps a clean and pleasant house, Mrs. Hudson, but her cooking can hardly be considered first-class.'

'Now, now, Holmes,' I laughed. 'Jealousy over a boiled egg doesn't quite become you.'

'Huh!'

I knew, of course, that Holmes's fit of pique was largely meant to be humorous. Our landlady, of whom we were both very fond, may not have had the range of menu provided by Simpson's but it was more than ample for our humble needs. Between us, we paid £210 per year for our rooms and, for such money, the cuisine was perfectly acceptable, perhaps even a little on the side of luxury.

Holmes got to his feet and, removing his black briar pipe from the pocket of his dressing gown, wandered across the room to the fireplace, where a store of his favourite tobacco was permanently kept hanging from the mantle in the toe-end of an odd Persian slipper.

'I shall content myself with a pipe of Bradley's finest. Perhaps Mrs. Hudson can make you up some sandwiches with those eggs of mine. It will save you having to close the surgery for lunch.'

It was as I was about to respond somewhat disfavourably to that suggestion that the distant cry of a newspaper vendor could first be heard emanating up from the street below.

'MURDER!'

Holmes's attention was immediately caught. He walked over to the window and lifted it open, sending a cool February breeze blowing through the room.

'Holmes, please!' I protested, having not yet attached my collar.

The newspaper vendor called out once more, his disturbing cry causing me to pause briefly as I lifted the tea cup to my lips.

'MURDER! READ ALL ABOUT IT! MUTILATED REMAINS FOUND IN THAMES!'

Holmes closed the window and paced across the sitting room to the door.

'At last! Something worth reading about!'

It need not be said that I failed to share my friend's enthusiasm for such matters. One of the things I first noted about Holmes after our first week lodging together was his vast knowledge of sensational crimes. There seemed hardly an act of infamy or terror that he couldn't provide immense details of at an instant, the most lurid of which seemed to be deliberately withheld until we were halfway through dinner. Many a time I have flung my cutlery down in annoyance and admonished Holmes for discussing such things while I was chewing on a piece of liver. He would simply laugh in response, beg my forgiveness and assure me such an incident would never occur again. Until the next time.

Hearing Holmes tear down the stairs, I got up from the table and wandered over to one of the two large bow windows that overlooked Baker Street. I was in time to see him dart out into the road and collect a newspaper from the vendor. He seemed oblivious to the stares he received from those pedestrians out at such an early hour, a man in his dressing gown hardly a frequent sight on London streets, most notably by an elderly woman who resorted to turning her head as she walked past him, a decision she soon came to regret after unfortunately wandering straight into the nearest lamp-post. Holmes returned briefly into the hall, having realised his failure to take any money with him. Mrs. Hudson kept a tray of small coins on a shelf just inside the front door for tipping tradesmen and delivery boys and I deduced it was this into which Holmes had dug for payment.

'It seems a body was pulled out of the water in the early hours, Watson,' my friend called out as he made his way back up the stairs. 'A man in middle-age, approximately five feet ten inches in height and of slim build. His body appears to have been mutilated in several places.'

'I haven't yet finished my breakfast,' said I, returning to the table. 'I would appreciate it if you withheld the more distressing details until I have finished.'

'I am afraid there is little more to divulge,' Holmes replied, casting the newspaper across the room. 'The editor clearly got wind of it just before going to press. There is nothing quite like the cry of 'Murder!' to sell newspapers, Watson, even if the corresponding article contains little by way of actual data.'

'Well, if you don't want it, I'll take it

with me,' I said. 'I can read it on my way to the surgery.'

'Please, be my guest.' Holmes deposited himself on the couch and breathed a long and heavy sigh. 'The London criminal has become boring and predictable. They do not consider their work an art, Watson, which it undoubtedly is.'

'Crime? An art? Come, Holmes, surely you're jesting!'

'Not at all. Like all other professions, if the common criminal approached his business with a certain degree of thought and dedication, who knows what heights he may scale. The prisons in this country are full of the most unambitious of fellows. If they had set their minds to it, they could have swapped their cells for mansions, their gruel for roasted pheasant in honey sauce and the cockchafer for a day at the races. All I do know, however, is that the only matters that have been brought to my attention recently have been unanimous in their banality.'

It was indeed true that Holmes's services had not been in great demand since the conclusion of the Copper

Beeches case the previous summer. A few matters of interest had come his way in the intervening months but he considered them all unworthy of his talents, quickly forming what turned out to be the correct conclusion in each affair in his mind before our callers had largely even finished telling their tales. It was a state of affairs I had been thinking about for some time. Inactivity for Holmes meant increased use of the cocaine bottle and I was anxious to prevent his reliance on such a drug spiralling towards addiction.

'Perhaps you should consider advertising your services in the agony columns?' I suggested.

Holmes sat bolt upright in the couch.

'Strike that thought from your mind!' he demanded. 'Do you wish me to be inundated with requests for finding lost dogs and runaway maids? Never!'

'Then perhaps you will allow me to write up the Jefferson Hope affair for publication.'

'Oh, I see,' Holmes said, rising from the comfort of the chair and returning to the table. 'We are onto that subject again, are we?'

'I honestly cannot see your objections,' I argued. 'The case was five years ago and is hardly a private matter. Even Lestrade has dined out on it. It's about time you took the credit.'

'My work is my own reward,' Holmes countered. 'I do not wish to see my likeness adorning the racks of railway booksellers.'*

'In that case, I see no other alternative for you than to mope around here all day waiting for the knock on the door that will never come.' I downed my remaining tea in one gulp and got to my feet. 'All businesses need publicity, Holmes. I see no reason why yours should be an exception.'

'I am a consulting detective, Watson!' Holmes's voice followed me as I left the sitting room and headed upstairs to my own private chamber. 'I do not solicit work! Clients are supposed to consult me, not the other way around!'

'Have it your own way!'

By the time I had attended to my toilet,

attached my collar and tie and returned downstairs, Holmes had moved once more. This time, he was seated on the armchair nearest the window, gazing out into the world beyond and puffing away at a fresh pipe. When he had no focus in life, Holmes could indeed become very difficult to live with. His reluctance to stay in one place for more than a minute was one of the less agreeable of his habits.

'Why don't you come with me, Holmes?' I said. 'If we leave now, we can go via the Yard. You could offer your help to Lestrade regarding the body in the Thames.'

'Alas, it does not come under his division,' Holmes replied. 'The body was found further east, near a landing stage by the Sugar plant at Victoria Dock. That would bring it under Inspector Jones's domain and, though I have never met the man, from what I can gather, he does not rate my methods too highly.'

'All the more reason to prove your worth.'

'I refuse to go cap in hand to Scotland Yard for employment, Watson. Many of my more interesting cases to date have been those which do not fall within the official force's remit. Take the Stoner case, for instance, or that dreadful business with the Abernetty family.'

'Ah, the butter and the parsley,' I chuckled. 'How could I possibly forget?'

'If the people concerned in those affairs had approached an officer of the law with their concerns, what would have happened? Nothing. There was no proof that Miss Stoner's life was in danger and the death of Ormond Abernetty had already been declared by a coroner as being of natural causes. I am the last court of appeal for such people, Watson.'

I collected my hat and coat from the stand and made to bid Holmes farewell for the day when, to my surprise, he tapped out his pipe and jumped to his feet.

'A change of scenery, though, may prove conducive to my spirits,' he said. 'If I can indulge upon you to wait a matter of three minutes while I dress, I will take up your offer of a shared hansom.'

Holmes was true to his word and returned from his bedroom in the stated time. He was not clad in the clothing I expected, however, choosing to don a rather coarse grey suit that had clearly seen better days. His hair also remained unbrushed.

'The state of my toilet is not appropriate for anything finer,' he explained, noting my expression of bewilderment. 'I would require a shave and a wash and I do not wish to deprive those poor souls who require your medical touch for a single moment longer than I have to.'

'Well, for heaven's sake, please try and avoid polite company,' said I. 'And where did you get that, Holmes? It smells something awful!'

'I picked it up off a barrow in the Curtain Road for a shilling.'

'You were robbed.'

'Anything else and I would stand out. I intend spending the day in the company of the less salubrious folk of the East End.'

I disapproved of such a venture but

knew it would be futile to express such sentiments. I was aware Holmes visited the slum areas of the city quite frequently, the observation of human beings in their natural habitat proving as interesting a hobby to him as those who watch birds.

'Well, be careful,' I said. 'Do you wish to take my revolver?'

'No, I don't believe that will be necessary. I am hardly a stranger in those parts. The landlord of the Cutler's Arms, a former professional bruiser by the name of Skinner, has known me for some years now. Or rather he has known Michael Kimble, known to all as Mack, late of Her Majesty's Navy and now gainfully employed as a groom by the Green Atlas Omnibus Company. Hence the smell. I drop in every now and then, catch up on the local gossip.'

'I'm sure you find it rewarding,' I commented. 'Come, let us leave.'

'After you, my dear fellow, after you. I feel certain, dressed like this, you will have more luck in hailing a cab than I.'

We left the house, after first popping our heads briefly into the parlour to compliment Mrs. Hudson on breakfast, and stood on the pavement outside for what seemed an eternity waiting for a hansom.

'Oh, the infernal nuisance of it!' I cried.

At that moment, a cab turned into the street from Portman Square.

'We appear to be in luck, said Holmes. 'Note how the passenger is folding away his newspaper. Clearly he is preparing to depart.'

The cab pulled to the side of the road and slowly inched its way along the kerb, the driver checking the property numbers to ensure he stopped outside the required address. To my amazement, the vehicle drew to a halt directly where we were standing and the passenger, a smartly dressed young man of approximately five-and-twenty years, duly alighted. He handed a coin up to the driver and, stepping around myself and Holmes, made for our very own front door, upon which he proceeded to knock.

'Cab, sir?' the driver asked down.

'What? Oh, yes. Thank you.'

I climbed aboard and looked back,

expecting to see Holmes follow me. His attention had instead moved to the young gentleman.

'Can I be of any assistance?'

'I have a letter for the attention of a Mr. Sherlock Holmes.'

Holmes held out his hand. 'Then allow me to relieve you of it.'

'I was instructed to hand it to Mr. Holmes personally,' the caller replied, with a marked air of self-importance. 'So if you intend taking it from me, my good man, and earning yourself a copper for delivering it, you are sadly mistaken.'

The door then opened and Mrs. Hudson appeared upon the threshold.

'Ah, good day to you, madam. I wish to see Mr. Sherlock Holmes.'

'Then you'd better turn around,' responded our landlady, 'for he is standing just behind you.'

The man did indeed turn back, though slowly and with more than a little embarrassment. He produced a narrow buff envelope from the inner pocket of his coat and handed it to Holmes.

'Forgive my impertinence, sir,' he said, rather meekly.

'Not at all,' said Holmes with good grace. 'Conduct yourself with such professionalism at all times and you will surely rise from the lowly position of Government clerk you currently occupy.'

I could tell from the look on the young man's face that he was surprised at Holmes's correct theory as to his occupation. I made a mental note to ask him how he had come to his conclusions for, as far as I could see, there was nothing obvious that suggested the gentlemen, who introduced himself as Simon Eversham, was in the employ of the civil service.

From my view in the hansom cab, the envelope which Holmes was now studying prior to opening appeared to have a red wax seal marked with an ornamental M. Though I did not know it at the time, the letter was from Holmes's brother, Mycroft, whom I did not meet until the case of the Greek Interpreter some two years later. It may seem strange to those reading my chronicles that, despite sharing diggings together for more than five years at that point, I was unaware of Holmes's elder sibling. It was not such a curious matter. We rarely discussed families, save to say both sets of parents had passed away, and indeed I also had an elder brother whose existence was equally unknown to Holmes.*

Holmes took out the letter and quickly read through its contents, which appeared to be nothing more than a couple of hastily scrawled lines.

'Are we leaving or not?' I queried, checking my watch.

'I fear you will have to proceed without me, Watson. The knock on the door that never comes has preferred, in this instance, to send a letter.'

'A request for your services?'

Holmes folded the letter and envelope in two and placed them both in the side pocket of his suit jacket.

'We shall see. Cabby, kindly take my friend to Chadwell Street and return for me. Mr. Eversham and I will be ready to leave for Whitehall in thirty minutes.'

'Yes, sir.'

The driver took up the reins, spurred on by the promise of an extra fare, and the cab moved off with a lurch towards Marylebone Road. I looked back to see Holmes and the young clerk step through the door of 221b. Despite there being those in desperate need of my ministration, I was momentarily impelled to ask the driver to stop and to rush back to my friend's side.

It was at moments like these, when the scent of a new adventure was fresh in the air, that Holmes was in his element. His enthusiasm was infectious and one could be carried along with it like a wave.

For all my desires, I had promised myself to the care of Templeton's patients and remained a man of my word. Ruing the fact that I had neglected to bring either of the newspapers, I settled back into the cab for the journey to Clerkenwell. My heart may have been in my duties as a doctor but, until I returned to Baker Street that evening and my curiosity as to the affair was satisfied, I knew my mind would be elsewhere.

2

Mercifully, my fourth day at the Chadwell Street surgery proved rather less demanding than those that had proceeded it. I had seen all of the patients that queued for my services by late afternoon and, after three home visits in the Clerkenwell and Islington areas, none of which fortunately proved too serious, I was back in Baker Street by six o'clock. Sherlock Holmes was nowhere to be seen and Mrs. Hudson, bringing me a welcome pot of tea before I had even had time to unlace my boots, informed me that he had not returned since leaving the house half an hour after me that morning.

It was to be another two hours before Holmes finally walked into our shared lounge, immediately discarding his hat and coat and practically collapsing into his favourite chair by the fire. I had finally instructed Mrs. Hudson to serve dinner for one, not knowing when, if at all,

Holmes would be returning that evening, and it was halfway through an excellent dish of curried fowl that he turned up.

'Ah, Watson, my dear fellow, you're back,' he said. 'I assume you've had a pleasant day at the surgery as the level in the whisky decanter has not dropped since this morning, unlike the three previous days when it was your first port of call upon arriving home.'

'Very reasonable, all things considered,' smiled I. 'Have you eaten?'

'A light lunch earlier, that will suffice for the moment. I do not think my stomach can take further food just yet, seeing as how I have just spent the best part of half an hour in the morgue of the Charing Cross Hospital. The stench of death has a nasty habit of remaining in the gullet long after leaving the premises.'

'The morgue, eh?'

'Examining the body of one Gianluca Carletti, Watson, late envoy of the Italian Government. It was his body fished out of the Thames in the early hours.'

'Indeed! And what, pray, is your involvement?'

'I have been commissioned to investigate the circumstances of his death.' Holmes stood up and selected his best clay from the assortment of pipes on the mantelpiece, which he proceeded to fill and light. 'Naturally, there is an official police investigation underway, under Athelney Jones's charge, but with the powers-that-be shutting up like a clam at the merest whiff of scandal, as people in their position are frequently wont to do, I fear they will not get far. I, on the other hand, spent an interesting lunch with a high-ranking civil servant and have been furnished with all available facts.'

Holmes returned to his seat, puffing silently on his pipe and sending bilious clouds of smoke into the air. Recognising his mood of reflectiveness, and keen to finish my meal before my appetite was ruined with talk of morgues and mutilated remains, I decided to wait until I was seated opposite him, enjoying my after-dinner pipe, before asking if he cared to share the details of the case.

'I suppose the Italian Embassy are pressing for answers, eh?'

'Hardly, they do not know,' Holmes replied. 'It appears Carletti was in London quite unofficially under the name of Buffón, making his own travel and accommodation arrangements.'

'Why the secrecy?'

'I shall take you into my confidence, my dear fellow. Carletti was here to initiate talks regarding a secret treaty between our two nations in the event of France gaining naval superiority over the Italians in the Mediterranean. He met with a representative of the Foreign Office and further talks were planned for today. He left the Whitehall Mansions Hotel, the venue for the talks, just before five last evening. The porter at Buxton's confirms Carletti arrived back there at around half-past and left again at eight, intending, so he said, to spend the evening at the theatre. He told the porter he would be back by eleven and that was the last anybody saw of him.'

'And what did you learn from examining the body?'

'That he died from a single stab-wound to the lower abdomen, piercing the flesh at an angle between the fourth and fifth ribs and travelling up to the heart. Though his watch, wallet and jewellery were missing, this was clearly no robbery, Watson.'

'The items were taken as a blind, you mean?

'It is my opinion so. That and, of course, to make identification more difficult. And then you have the mutilations. Dozens of deep slashes executed with an extremely sharp knife, the blade some seven inches long with a serrated edge, both horizontally and vertically across the abdomen from the neck to the groin. It is nothing like I have ever seen before.'

'Another blind? To make it appear Carletti was the victim of a frenzied attack? Or possibly it was intended as a warning to those who sent him on his secret mission?'

'Perhaps.'

Holmes got to his feet and made his way across the sitting room to the table, where he proceeded to pour himself a glass of water from the carafe that accompanied my meal. Though Mrs. Hudson served her curries much tamer than the dishes I became used to dining on during my military service in India, I nonetheless considered it advisable to have water within reach at all times.

'What else did you learn from the cadaver?'

'Only that Carletti was a married man, the faint band of untanned skin on his finger where the ring was removed enough to tell me that, was immaculate in his toilet, suffered from a slight goitre and was a habitual taker of snuff. His clothing provided more details of the precise circumstances of his death. The wounds could never have been inflicted with them *on* for they would be saturated in blood. They were not. Also his shoelaces had been tied by someone else.'

'He was attacked *naked*?' I asked incongruously.

'And his body dressed again before being dumped? Yes, I believe so.'

'So where will you begin?'

'I have already searched Carletti's hotel room and interviewed the Foreign Office official with whom he met. Neither, unfortunately, turned up anything of interest. Several leads still suggest themselves, however. I only returned for a short rest and a fresh pipe. I left in such a hurry this morning, the half an hour I allowed barely enough to attend to my toilet and change, that I went completely without my tobacco.'

'You're going out again now?'

'Yes.' Holmes downed the remainder of the water in one and headed into his private chamber. 'Under normal circumstances, I would, of course, ask you to accompany me. I trust, on this occasion, you would be forced to decline?'

I cursed my ill fortune and, ashamed though I am to admit it, the thought of abandoning Templeton's patients did momentarily cross my mind. My duty, however, came first and, much as I enjoyed being involved with Holmes's investigations, in truth, I would not have wanted it any other way.

'I could perhaps spare you an hour or two, Holmes, but I cannot possibly stay out too late.'

'No, no, my dear fellow,' came the reply, 'I wouldn't hear of it. I'm likely to remain away for some time and you need your sleep. Don't trouble yourself over it.'

'But there's one thing I do not understand, Holmes. If Signór Carletti's body was only recovered in the early hours of this morning and with no identification on his person, how were Whitehall so quick to hear of it?'

'Carletti was reported missing by the duty manager of the Buxton Hotel last night, it being their policy to inform the local beat constable of any guests who are unaccounted for when the doors are locked by the night-porter at midnight, especially those who are strangers to the city. The constable informed his station sergeant when finishing his beat and a description of the missing man, whom they believed to be a wealthy Italian businessman and a natural target for the parasites that plague our streets, was passed to the Yard.

'The body was recovered from the Thames by two dock-workers at dawn, it having become tangled with a marker-buoy, and, as it was clear to the local bobby who was called to the scene to be an obvious case of robbery and murder, Inspector Jones was called in. The description of the body matched that of the missing Signór Buffón and the connection made. The manager of the Buxton was called in to identify the body, which he did, and a telegram was despatched to a contact address left by Carletti at the hotel. Ostensibly, and as far as Jones still believes, the head office of his business in Rome, it in fact was a box for the Italian Foreign Service. They contacted Whitehall, the body was swiftly moved to the morgue of the Charing Cross Hospital and I was brought in.

'From the body first being seen in the water to my summons, all within the space of two hours. I may criticise such institutions as Scotland Yard and Whitehall at times, Watson, but as organisations, when they put their collective minds to it, they are capable of work of the highest order.'

Sherlock Holmes emerged from his bedroom clothed in the same drab moth-eaten grey suit he had donned briefly that morning. His jet-black hair, which was normally worn combed neatly back, had been ruffled and a touch of theatrical make-up had been applied to his face to give a weather-beaten appearance.

'The eponymous Michael Kimble will take over from here,' he said. 'For the body to have been washed up at Victoria Dock, there are only a small number of places it can have been deposited into the water. Low-tide was just before one this morning so it was likely to have been from a landing stage, possibly around the area of Bugsby's Reach, than merely dumped over the embankment wall. Several possibilities suggest themselves. I will merge into the background far more successfully dressed like this.'

Holmes checked his appearance in the large mirror that hung above the mantelpiece and, after making one or two minor adjustments, declared himself ready for the task ahead.

'On this occasion, Watson, I fear it will be necessary to take your revolver with me, if the offer of this morning still stands. I do not anticipate trouble but it would be foolish to go unprepared for it.'

'By all means.' I got to my feet and collected my trusted revolver from the drawer of my desk. Disappointed as I was not to be accompanying him, knowing that he carried the Webley★ made me feel infinitely better. I loaded six cartridges into the chamber. 'And your first port of call is Bugsby's Reach?'

'I merely wish to see the location under similar light, or rather the lack of it, as the perpetrator of this horrific crime had when they sought to dispose of the body. Hopefully, further avenues of investigation will result. There will no doubt be a number of public houses nearby and possibly a cab-rank or two. Information is what I seek. The revolver is a last resort, Watson, my weapon of choice is a pocket of half-crowns.' Holmes took the Webley and placed it into his pocket. 'I shall be off. You get a good night's sleep, my dear fellow, and I shall see you at breakfast. Tell Mrs. Hudson to serve bacon. Unlike her soft boiled eggs, that is one thing I always find she can cook to perfection.'

* * *

Perfect though they may have been, the rashers on Sherlock Holmes's breakfast plate soon got cold.

'Staying out in all that weather will be the death of him,' Mrs. Hudson remarked as she began to clear the table. 'It didn't stop teeming down till well after four, you know.'

'I'm sure he would've sought shelter, Mrs. Hudson,' I replied.

It was typical of Holmes to miss the meal, despite making arrangements to the contrary, though this time, of course, it was different. Holmes was trawling the warren of streets in London's docklands looking for a brutal murderer and his non-appearance troubled me enormously. It was nearly eight o'clock and I had delayed my leaving for Chadwell Street as late as possible, hoping Holmes would turn up. I tore a sheet from my desk journal, scribbled a note for him to send word to me at the surgery as soon as he arrived back in Baker Street, save I should worry all day, and gathered together my things.

As I stood waiting for a cab, I bought a *Daily Telegraph* from a passing vendor. Holmes had a selection of London newspapers delivered daily to our rooms but, with him being a late riser and also preferring the later editions, as they contained more details of any news that had come in overnight, they did not usually arrive until well after nine. It was while I was glancing through the front page of the paper that a small headline halfway down the third column attracted my attention.

'DEVELOPMENTS IN THAMES MURDER CASE,' it read. 'INSPECTOR ATHELNEY JONES MAKES ARREST'.

As developments go, this was an unexpected one. With precious little to go on, and not being party to all of the facts, it was considered that Scotland Yard would have no success in the matter. I gave a further two blasts on my cab-whistle and, at last, a hansom came trumbling up. Settled in the back and on my way to the surgery, I read through the article. Though details were scant, it appeared a vagrant, well known to the local police, was picked up in possession of the wallet of Pietro Buffón, Carletti's alias, a property manager from Rome. The vagrant had pawned Carletti's pocket-watch and jewellery at a brokers in Roscoe Street, less than half a mile from Bugsby's Reach, three hours after the body was discovered. It was, I naturally assumed, standard procedure for all local pawnbrokers to be visited by officers when a crime involved the theft of such items.

The brokership in Roscoe Street, the article continued, confirmed they had taken receipt of an item of gold jewellery and a pocket-watch, both Italian in their style and manufacture, and the vagrant, instantly recognisable by the description given, was soon traced. With the wallet still in his possession, an arrest was made and, it was said, a charge of murder may soon follow.

A plausible theory, fitting the details provided in the report, could easily be formed. Carletti, or Buffón, a stranger to London, somehow became lost, possibly after enjoying an evening on the town, and was attacked by the vagrant. He was stripped of anything of value and his body dumped into the Thames. Holmes, however, was always keen to warn me of the dangers of such hypothesising and I, of course, knew more than the meagre facts given in the article. There were the mutilations for one and the curious fact put forward by Holmes that Carletti had been slain naked and then redressed. The location was also strange. The envoy was last seen in Whitehall and his hotel was on the Strand, yet he was apparently attacked in the vicinity of Victoria Dock, a good four or five miles away.

I pondered the various points these inconsistencies threw up as I continued my journey to the surgery, travelling along the Euston and Pentonville Roads into Clerkenwell. The queue of people along Chadwell Street swiftly eradicated all thoughts of the case from my mind. It was longer than it had ever been, even more so than that first Monday. As the cab drew to a halt at the kerbside, I steeled myself for the arduous day ahead.

It was gone two before I finally allowed myself half an hour to eat lunch, a ham sandwich prepared for me by Mrs. Hudson, and to smoke a pipe. A knock at the door interrupted my brief and, in my mind, well-earned sojourn and I angrily barked an order for them to wait. To my astonishment, the door swung open. I jumped to my feet, prepared if necessary to use force to eject the unwanted invader from the room, when Sherlock Holmes spoke.

'Forgive me for interrupting your lunch, my dear fellow. I can see you've had a trying morning.'

'Not at all, Holmes, come in!' I cried, mighty relieved to see my friend at last. 'My god, you look terrible.'

'It was a long night and I have yet to sleep. I returned to our lodgings to find your angry note and felt I had better throw myself on your mercy before taking a nap.'

'I did not consider it to be too strongly worded,' I replied. 'On the contrary, I felt it was quite polite under the circumstances.'

'Your words were the epitome of civility, Watson, as always, but the depth of the pencil strokes and the fact that you broke the point twice while writing indicated an underlying sense of asperity.'

'Well, I admit to being a touch aggrieved,' I said, 'but I had every justification for being concerned for your welfare. You were, after all, on the trail of a vicious murderer.'

'Then let us say no more about it.'

'Have you read the newspaper?' Sitting down, I pointed him towards my copy of the *Daily Telegraph*. 'It appears you may have underestimated Athelney Jones. He has made an arrest and, on the face of it, the evidence looks pretty damning.'

Holmes glanced briefly at the article in question.

'A vagrant did not commit this crime, Watson. No tramp worth his salt would have taken the man's wallet, watch and jewellery and left his shoes. Hand-made

41

of the finest Italian leather and, I surmise from the lack of scuff marks or wear upon the sole, bought by Carletti especially for this trip. They would fetch a pretty penny or two, I can tell you.'

'But why would a killer strip his victim before murdering him, only to dress him once more before disposing of the body?'

'The more clever the murderer, the more clever the crime, Watson. Attempts to conceal the identity of the victim, the taking of his possessions, is one thing, I would assume that of any murderer with an ounce of intelligence, but to set in motion a false trail of evidence leading towards a convenient scapegoat quite another. No, no, the vagrant is innocent, I have no doubt of that.'

'Hadn't you better inform Jones before he makes a charge?'

'The vagrant will be enjoying his stay in the hospitality of the Yard, Watson. A bed and a warm meal a day is more than he gets on the streets. No, I can afford to let Jones chase his own shadows for a few more days yet. The vagrant will not suffer any hardship.'

'So what did you learn from your night at Victoria Dock?'

'Precious little. Even at night, there is much traffic through the area; carts of all descriptions, merchants, labourers.'

'Did you learn nothing of interest?'

'I had a rather informative chat with an old wharfinger about the currents and tides around the area of Bugsby's Reach. If the corpse had not snagged on a buoy rope, it would have moved swiftly up river with the incoming tide and possibly not been found for days. Carletti may still have been identified, of course, but there would have been no clues as to where his body was deposited into the Thames. We have indeed been fortunate.'

'So what will you do now?'

'First, take to my bed. Though an investigation may seem to give me untold energy, I am not a bottomless well. I must sleep or face collapse through nervous exhaustion. I shall go out again this evening. There's one or two more things I wish to get clear in my mind before attempting to formulate a theory.'

'Do you still have the revolver?'

'No, I left it in Baker Street before coming here to set your mind at rest. But do not worry. I shall take it with me again this evening. While last night, I merely scratched the surface of the dark and murky world that lies behind the high wharves and warehouses of the Thames; tonight I intend to immerse myself deep into it.'

3

Sherlock Holmes was gone by the time I returned from the surgery, though that was not unexpected as it was past ten o'clock. I consoled myself with the thought that tomorrow, being a Saturday, was only half-day at the surgery and I would then be free of my burden of care to enjoy the rest of the weekend. After a light supper and, something that Holmes had previously noted, a generous serving from the whisky decanter, I retired for the night.

Rising and breakfasting before eight-thirty, surgery on a Saturday not beginning until half past nine, I was not at all surprised to learn that Holmes had once again stayed out all night and was yet to return. Leaving the house at nine o'clock on the dot, again buying a morning paper to read on the journey, though there was no mention of any further police developments in the case, I travelled directly to

Chadwell Street and opened the doors to the throng of unfortunates that lined the pavement. The fact this was the last chance to get medical attention for two days brought many extra people out of the woodwork, far too many to see in just a morning surgery, but I resolved to finish my consultations at one o'clock sharp as I needed to call in at the Post Office before returning to Baker Street.

The only income the surgery had was in the selling of various medicines, tonics and ointments. Most were issued free, courtesy of Templeton's wealthy sponsors, but, for those who could afford it, a mere twopence would acquire a bottle of *McCoy's Health Tonic*, a general restorative that was said to cure, according to the claims of the manufacturer on the label, *all manner of aches, pains and ailments*. Templeton told me he took around fifteen to twenty shillings a week in this way, though the medicine he dispensed was worth at least five times that. My first week in charge of the surgery had brought in the grand total of four shillings and sixpence. I understood from Templeton that a few patients, strangers to me, might plead poverty in the hope of getting free medicine where he, for the most part, knew those who were able to contribute a little to the cost of their care. Nevertheless, I was a little disturbed by the low funds and, not wishing to let Templeton or his sponsors down, added a little of my own allowance before banking it.

Most of the illnesses I saw at the surgery were a result of malnutrition or poor sanitation. It was remarkable just how few of the patients were actually *ill*, considering the conditions in which they lived. Only one in five had shoes on their feet and an even less number than that could claim to have had a decent meal in the past week. It was hard to believe we were in the very heart of the richest and most civilised nation on Earth.

The morning passed reasonably quickly and without too much incident. I bolted the doors, despite the theatrics of those still waiting, at one o' clock as planned and returned to Baker Street via the Holborn branch of the Post Office, where the total of twelve shillings was happily deposited in the surgery's account. Sherlock Holmes sat at the table, wearing the mouse-coloured dressing gown that had my gift to him on the occasion of his birthday the month before. He was tucking heartily into a meat and potato pudding.

'You have finished for the week, I take it, Watson? Ring the bell, my dear fellow, and Mrs. Hudson will bring you up your share of this delicious meal. You look as though you are in need of as much sustenance as I.'

'Have you been back long?' I asked, hanging up my hat and coat.

'A mere two minutes after you had left this morning by all accounts. I immediately retired to my bed and have been awake no longer than the time it took you to drive here from the Holborn Post Office.'

'How on earth did you know I came home via Holborn?'

'A magician loses all regard when he explains his tricks,' Holmes replied. 'He comes across as a mere charlatan where, only moments before, he was held in awe. Allow me just this once, my dear fellow, to retain a feeling of the latter.'

'Very well.' I agreed, laughing, as I rang the bell and took my seat at the table. 'Do you have any further news about Carletti's murder?'

'I'm afraid I learned little more last night, Watson, despite my endeavours. I believe a cart or growler must have been used to transport the body to the river's edge, for I can find nobody who saw anything out of the ordinary, but, save for that, I am being frustrated at every turn. It is the motive that troubles me.'

'There must be many who would be opposed to a possible naval treaty between England and Italy, I suggested, international politics being what it is, and would seek to throw a spanner in the works.'

'But Carletti's visit here was a mere preliminary,' replied Holmes. 'He was just a pawn, Watson, preparing the board ahead of the introduction of the more powerful and influential pieces. Apart from three or four people in the Ministry and their counterparts in Italy, not a living soul knew Gianluca Carletti was in London.'

'And yet he was murdered in such a way that, eliminating a random street attack for his valuables, could only suggest some sort of warning to his superiors?'

'I am not convinced.'

'So what will you do now?' I asked.

'Continue my efforts, Watson. What more can I do?' said Holmes. 'If the body was, as I suggest, transported to the Thames by growler, the actual scene of the crime could be anywhere. No, I fear, unless Lady Fortune smiles down on us once more, my labours will be in vain. This may have to go down as a case I could not crack.'

'And the vagrant? What will happen if you fail to find the evidence to clear him?'

'Then he will hang.'

It was a sobering thought and I sensed there might soon be a change in the focus of Holmes's investigation. Instead of trying to discover the identity of Carletti's killer and the motive behind it, it may soon have to be enough just to provide sufficient evidence to persuade Inspector Jones they had the wrong man. A vagrant the arrested man might have been but he, as much as Gianluca Carletti, deserved justice.

The door opened at that moment and Mrs. Hudson appeared with a tray.

'Your lunch, Doctor.'

'Ah, splendid!'

Mrs. Hudson placed the steaming plate in front of me as I rubbed my hands together with glee. I do not consider myself prone to exaggeration when I say a week at the Chadwell Street surgery had caused a good two pound weight loss and, with Mrs. Hudson's help, I was determined to put it all back on again before the weekend was out.

'And the last edition of the *Daily Gazette*.'

Holmes took the proffered newspaper with scant acknowledgement. I recognised this blackness he was slowly sinking into. He took his failings in his work seriously and personally, believing always that it was down to something he alone had missed or overlooked.

51

The meat and potato pudding looked and smelled delicious and a single mouthful was hardly enough to satisfy my princely appetite. That was all I managed to have before Holmes leapt to his feet and stormed across the room to his chamber.

'Plaistow, Watson! We leave immediately!'

'What's going on?'

'Mrs. Hudson, a cab at the door in one minute, if you would be so kind!'

'Holmes . . .'

'Stay if you wish, Watson, stay if you wish!'

'No, no, I will come if you want me to but can it not at least wait until we've finished our lunch.'

'Time is of the essence!'

Holmes reappeared with his clothes thrown untidily on over his nightshirt and, collecting his hat and coat from the stand, made out onto the landing. I removed the napkin from my lap, it having been there all of thirty seconds, and hurried to my feet.

'Why Plaistow? Holmes, will you stop for one moment and tell me what on earth is going on?'

Holmes paused briefly on the landing and looked back at me through the open sitting room door. The dark mood had lifted and there was a gleam of excitement in his eyes.

'Another murder, Watson!' he said. 'Another murder!'

★ ★ ★

The weather had taken another turn for the worse and our journey to the Plaistow district of the city was through torrential rain and wind. Holmes was furious.

'Vital evidence may be washed completely away!' he bemoaned. 'Lady Fortune may be on our side, Watson, but Mother Nature is assuredly working against us!'

'I take it you saw something of interest in the *Daily Gazette*?'

'A report of a body found in the Marsh Lane area of Plaistow. Male, early to mid-thirties, well dressed but with no identification upon his person. His torso appeared to show signs of extensive mutilation.'

'My word! And you suppose there may be a connection?'

'That has yet to be ascertained. My, this weather really is terrible! God speed, driver, and there's an extra half-crown in it for you!'

★　★　★

The downpour had reduced to a slight drizzle by the time we arrived at the entrance to Marsh Lane. A constable stood on the corner of the street and, as we climbed down from the cab, he and Holmes immediately acknowledged each other.

'Ah, Constable Andrews, is it not?'

'Why, Mr. Holmes, sir! Good to see you.'

'Can you tell us what has gone on here, Andrews?'

'A body was found in one of the yards, sir, 'bout seven this morning.'

'Is it still there?'

'No, sir, it's been removed to the mortuary. Inspector Jones has just arrived to look the area over. I'm to wait here, he said, and not let anybody into the street till he's finished.'

'I see.'

Holmes guided me away from the constable where we could talk without being overheard.

'Did you hear that? Jones has obviously sensed a connection between the two crimes. This is K division, Inspector Toller's patch, and Jones would have no reason to come here otherwise.'

'Toller?'

'I've met him once and, without wishing to blow my own trumpet, impressed him enormously over an insignificant deduction concerning his wife's penchant for baked apple and sugar tarts. It may have proven useful after all. Ah, talk of the devil, here they come. Toller, my good man!'

Inspector Toller, a small fellow with a full black beard, came walking up the lane, accompanied by whom I correctly assumed to be Athelney Jones of H division.★

'Mr. Holmes, what brings you this far out of town?' Toller inquired. 'Heard about our little murder, have you?'

'It has one or two small points of interest.'

The cough that emanated from Inspector Jones at that point was almost enough to scare the birds from the nearby trees, let alone remind Toller of his presence.

'Oh, allow me to introduce you, Jones. This is Mr. Sherlock Holmes, a name that echoes along the corridors of Scotland Yard from time to time.'

'Greetings, Inspector,' beamed my friend, extending his hand. 'I do not believe we've had the pleasure of working together?'

'No,' came the stiff reply, though the hand was accepted as a matter of common courtesy. 'And I'll tell you now, Mr. Holmes, I do not approve of private detective agents and their interference in police matters. Kindly remove yourself from the vicinity, you'll get no change here.'

'You are in charge of this investigation?' asked Holmes.

'This is official police business and I'm warning you to make yourself scarce, sir.'

'Surely that is Toller's prerogative. Toller, you wouldn't have any objections to myself and my colleague Doctor Watson taking a look along the lane, would you? The body has, after all, been removed and you have both searched the area. There is nothing with which we can interfere.'

'Very well,' agreed Toller. 'I suppose there's no harm in it.'

'On your head be it,' Jones said to his colleague. 'Police work is a highly skilled business and allowing amateurs to run roughshod over an investigation will only lead to trouble.'

'I have no intention of running roughshod over anything or anyone,' Holmes responded. 'Anything of interest I may discover will, of course, be passed onto the proper authorities without delay. I have no wish to hinder your inquiries.'

Jones, a stout man with a flushed face, scoffed loudly and strode off towards a waiting police carriage.

'I take it you will be releasing the vagrant?'

Jones looked briefly back at Holmes but did not reply. He boarded the carriage and barked at the driver to move on.

'Alas, our good Inspector Jones bears a

heavy burden,' Holmes commented. 'He must now look again at the Thames killing, an investigation he, his superiors and, more importantly perhaps, the press had considered closed.' Holmes turned his attention to Toller. 'Now, Inspector Toller, where was the body found?'

'About a hundred yards along on your left, Mr. Holmes,' Toller explained, pointing us towards a range of small industrial buildings set a short distance back from the road, in the yard of one Josiah Rumney. 'That's him outside with the spotted neckerchief.'

'Any leads as to the victim's identity?'

'None as yet, apart from the fact he seemed a well dressed gent. From what I gathered from Jones, the body in the Thames was also stripped of any personal belongings. Fortunately, they happened to have a report of a missing person come in at the same time and the descriptions tallied. We may be equally fortuitous.'

'Let us hope so, Toller. Would you care to accompany us?'

'No, I've a few matters to attend to

here then I'll be heading back to the station.'

'Until we meet again, then. Come, Watson.'

★ ★ ★

Marsh Lane was a long L shaped road on the outskirts of the district and located close to the intersection of the North Woolwich and the London, Tilbury & Southend railway lines. It was bordered on one side by several rows of small warehouses and a foundry and by smallholdings and a livery stable on the other.

'Mr. Josiah Rumney?'

Rumney sat on a small barrel outside the entrance to his yard, rolling a cigarette. He looked up as we approached.

'Aye.'

'My name is Sherlock Holmes, this is my colleague Doctor Watson. The body was discovered in your yard, I believe?'

'Found it meself,' replied Rumney. 'Gave me the willies, it did.'

'Quite. And what type of business do

you run from these premises?'

'Animal feed, straw, manure.'

The third of the items on the list I had already guessed from the festering smell. The wooden gates of the yard were open and I could see the cause of the powerful odour; a pile of fresh horse-dung some six feet high.

'And it was about seven o'clock, I understand?'

'That's right. I only came in to supervise an extra delivery of manure and there he was in the corner.'

'You do not normally work on a Saturday, then?'

'Graft bleedin' 'ard enough durin' the week to sweat it out at weekends an' all,' replied Rumney. 'I usually take the family out for the day. Look, it's almost bleedin' three o'clock now! My name'll be mud when I get 'ome and that's no lie!'

'Well, Mr. Rumney, I believe Inspector Toller has finished here for the moment so I don't imagine he will object to you being on your way. Will you allow us a brief look inside your yard before you go?'

'Be me guest, mate. Watch where

you're treading, though, won't you?'

Holmes and I entered the yard, which in turn led into a small storehouse full of sacks of animal meal and bundles of straw, and looked the place over. There was no sign of where the body once lay.

'If the mutilations were anything like those on Carletti's torso, there would have been considerable blood loss. There is nothing here at all. Again, this is just a dumping ground, not the scene of the crime. Did you note Rumney saying he doesn't normally work at weekends? Those who deposited the body over the fence didn't expect it to be found until Monday morning at the earliest.'

'Which implies some knowledge of Rumney's business?' I suggested.

'Indeed.' While I took a look inside the storehouse, Holmes walked systematically around the yard, hands behind his back and with his head down, carefully examining every inch of the cobble-stoned surface. 'The rain has turned the lane outside into a real quagmire. That, and the amount of traffic that has passed along there this morning, has made it impossible for me to identify the tracks of the vehicle that brought the victim here. It is no better inside the yard. This surface allows no traces or indentations of any kind to be made.'

'A cigarette butt, Holmes!' I cried out in triumph. 'There!'

'Yes, I saw it. Hand-rolled with cheap paper and even cheaper tobacco. It is one of Rumney's. No, there is nothing here for us. We may have better luck at the mortuary. An unidentified body in K division would be taken where, in your experience, Watson?'

'The East Ham Hospital?' I advised. 'Or perhaps the local workhouse morgue?'

'I think the hospital,' replied Holmes. 'We're not dealing with a tramp found face down in the gutter, our victim was a well dressed man. Which is something else he had in common with Carletti. Come, we can no doubt blag ourselves in to see the cadaver.'

★　★　★

Sherlock Holmes and I picked up a hansom at the entrance to the lane, both Inspector Toller and Constable Andrews having since departed, and journeyed to East Ham Hospital, a ride of some fifteen minutes. The mortuary had indeed taken receipt of the Marsh Lane corpse and we were able to gain access with little fuss. As soon as I had introduced myself as a doctor, a helpful attendant showed us into the basement mortuary and directly to the cadaver in question. I later learned they were expecting a police surgeon from H division, one who has examined the body of Gianluca Carletti and had been asked by Inspector Jones to offer his expert opinion as to whether the same hand was responsible for both deaths. Holmes was in no doubt.

'Yes, the mutilations are almost identical,' he told me as we examined the corpse. 'And note the knife wound between the fourth and fifth ribs.'

'Dear god!' I cried, horrified at the extent and ferocity of the injuries. 'What man could have done this?'

'That is what we will hopefully find

out,' Holmes said. 'Cast your expert eye over him, Watson, while I take a look at the fellow's clothing.'

The victim's clothes had been removed and were arranged on a nearby table. Holmes examined them carefully with his lens while I saw to the corpse.

'The weapon is as you described,' I said. 'A blade seven to perhaps eight inches long with a serrated edge.'

'Splendid. Anything else?'

'Well, yes,' I ventured to suggest, slightly hesitant in case I was simply drawing Holmes's attention to something he had already taken note of, as I was often unfortunately inclined to do. 'There is something curious.'

Holmes was at my side in a moment.

'Take a look.' I pointed him towards a thin cut running horizontally across the man's torso, hardly visible among the thick coagulated blood that caked his chest. 'Do you see this laceration here? It was made with a different knife, I would swear to that. A thinner, far more delicate blade.'

Holmes quickly collected his lens from

the table and closely examined the thin cut. 'You have put me to shame, Watson!' he cried, throwing his arms into the air. 'We must leave for Charing Cross immediately!'

'Charing Cross?'

'Gianluca Carletti's body is bound for a ship leaving for Italy this very day! I only pray we are not too late!'

4

We raced out of the hospital, procured a cab and ordered the driver to spare nothing to get us to Charing Cross as quickly as possible. Holmes lit himself a pipe and spent the journey staring broodingly ahead. The silence was frustrating for me, anxious to know what my discovery had triggered but unwilling to add to his obvious vexation by asking him for an explanation. I decided instead to inquire on a different point.

'Did you learn anything from the victim's clothing?'

'Only that he was a solicitor, travelled into the city each day via Paddington Station and was a smoker of Turkish cigars, which he kept in a monogrammed leather case in his top right pocket,' Holmes answered. 'A brief examination of the corpse also informed me he was an exceedingly vain man and walked with a slight limp, perhaps caused by polio as a child. The two are, I would suggest, connected. I will wire those small facts to Toller and no doubt he will secure a positive identification.'

'He still had the cigar case on him, then?'

'No, it was missing.'

'Then how could you possibly . . .'

'The odour of Turkish tobacco is quite unique, Watson,' Holmes explained, 'as is that of leather. I clearly discerned both on the inner lining of the top right pocket.'

'But how on earth do you fathom the case was monogrammed?' I asked. 'Surely that is a leap too far even for you!'

'There would be no other reason to take it, unless it could be used to help identify the victim. His necktie was also missing, possibly for the same purpose. A vain man such as he was, the bottled colouring he used on his hair enough to tell me that, perhaps his initials were woven into the design.'

'And what about bloodstains?'

'Very few. The circumstances of his death are identical to that of Carletti.'

'But what possible connection could

there be between an Italian diplomat, in the country secretly to arrange terms of a meeting to discuss a possible naval treaty between our two nations, and a London solicitor?'

'That has yet to be discovered.'

Holmes put the stem of the pipe back to his lips and the remainder of the journey was spent in silence. The cab got us to the corner of Ludgate Hill quite quickly before the heavens opened once more and the rain slowed our progress. We eventually limped up to Charing Cross Hospital and hurried around to the rear entrance of the mortuary. A coffin was being loaded onto the back of a covered cart while Simon Eversham, the young Government clerk, supervised from the shelter of the doorway.

'Eversham! Do I take it that casket contains the body of Pietro Buffón?'

'Indeed it does, Mr. Holmes,' replied Eversham, unaware of the true identity of the deceased or the exact nature of the case. 'What brings you back here?'

'I wish to see the body one more time.'

'I'm afraid that will be quite impossible, Mr. Holmes. He's due on a train at Waterloo. There's a packet leaving Southampton bound for Italy at eleven this very night.'

'He will make his train,' said Holmes, 'but first I require one further examination. Kindly have him taken back into the mortuary.'

'Please, Mr. Holmes, I really cannot allow . . .'

'Eversham, if you wish to serve your superiors well, you will do as I ask,' said Holmes, politely but firmly. 'It is a matter of extreme importance!'

'Very well, if you insist. But the train leaves Waterloo at six-twelve and he needs to be on it. Otherwise, I shall be . . .'

'I will take full responsibility, you have no need to worry.'

After a nod from Eversham, the porters unloaded the coffin from the cart and took it back into the mortuary. It was placed upon a low table just inside the door and, upon Holmes's instructions, the lid was unscrewed. Gianluca Carletti lay inside, fully dressed and at peace. An undertaker had been called in to prepare the body for his return to his homeland and theatrical make-up had been applied to rid Carletti's skin of the pallor of death. Holmes unbuttoned the gentleman's coat, waistcoat and shirt to reveal the severe mutilations to his trunk. The body had been washed and the individual wounds were much clearer to the eye than those of the victim currently lying on a cold stone slab in East Ham.

'There!' cried Holmes, pointing to a thin laceration across Carletti's abdomen, running closely adjacent to and party obliterated by a far savage and deeper wound.

'It certainly appears similar,' I agreed. 'What on earth do you make of it?'

'What in the name of the devil is going on here!' Inspector Athelney Jones stood in the open doorway, looking into the anteroom with abject horror and anger. 'Mr. Holmes, this is an abomination, sir!'

'Ah, Inspector Jones . . . '

'You have absolutely no right to be here and even less to open that coffin! Have you no respect, man? My god, I'll have you hauled over the coals for this!'

'Good afternoon, Inspector,' Eversham piped up, producing some official-looking documentation from his attaché case. 'My name is Eversham and I am from the Foreign Office. I am here to supervise the return of Signór Buffón to his family in Italy.'

'Then you should have put a stop to this damn sacrilege! And as for you, Mr. Holmes, you could be facing a charge for this! You have absolutely no authority!'

'I think you'll find, Inspector,' I started, 'that Holmes has the highest authori . . . '

'That'll be fine, thank you, Watson,' Holmes interrupted me, 'we have seen all we came to see. Your co-operation was very much appreciated, Mr. Eversham.'

'By god, if I wasn't such a busy man, I'd run you in!' Jones hollered. 'And don't go thinking you can wrap Toller around your little finger anymore. For your information, I have just been assigned to the central office and have been put in charge of *both* investigations.

'Ah, you believe the same man to be responsible, then?'

'I have yet to form an opinion on that. Now, be off with you!'

'And you have released the vagrant?'

'That is a police matter and none of your concern,' said Jones. 'I'm warning you, Mr. Holmes, you'd better stay out of this affair otherwise you could well find yourself on Queer Street! Now, are you going to leave willingly or do I have to summon assistance to remove you by force?'

'We're going, sir!' I roared. 'Do not trouble yourself!'

Holmes and I left the mortuary with the sound of Jones admonishing young Eversham, reminding him of his responsibilities and threatening to report him to his superiors, ringing in our ears. I was furious about being ejected from the premises, as well as being spoken to in such a manner.

'The impudence of the man! He would do well to keep a civil tongue in his head! And why did you allow him to bully you in such a fashion, Holmes? You are acting on the authority of the British Government! You should have put him firmly in his place!'

'Calm yourself, my dear fellow,' said Holmes. 'We have far more important things to do than cross swords with Scotland Yard. Revealing my hand would inevitably mean revealing Carletti's true identity and it would soon reach the ears of a dozen newspaper editors. No, it has been a very successful visit, despite that rather unseemly altercation, and we now have several more leads to follow up.'

'Which are?'

'Firstly, Watson, the vagrant. He has been released all right, that was clear from Jones's tone, now we just have to locate him. He may not have murdered Carletti but he certainly got the man's possessions from somewhere.'

'There must be thousands of vagrants in London, Holmes, and I can't see Inspector Jones giving us the fellow's details.'

'They are creatures of habit, Watson,' Holmes replied. 'And as territorial as any wild animal. We shall find him around the area of Bugsby's Reach.'

We walked out of the hospital grounds and into the main throng of Charing

Cross Road. A light rain was still falling and with Baker Street a good twenty-minute walk and no sign of an available cab, we seized the moment to hop on a passing Green Atlas omnibus that would take us practically to our door.

'Tell me, Holmes,' I asked, 'what do you make of those strange wounds on both victims?' The question, unanswered before owing to Jones's untimely arrival on the scene, seemed to trouble Holmes. Indeed, I had taken note of his expression when he first saw the cut on Carletti's torso. It was one of anger that he had failed to notice it before, though if the condition of the body on his first visit to the Charing Cross mortuary was anything like that of the Marsh Lane victim, he could hardly be blamed. Neither of them were very deep. Hardly piercing the skin, in fact.

'Speculation at this stage is unhelpful,' Holmes replied, 'and may only serve to cloud my judgement. Ah, conductor? Two to Baker Street, please.'

'So what do we do next?'

'I have business to attend to at the

telegraph office, then I suggest we enjoy a decent supper before heading out to Victoria Dock.'

'From the *we*, I take it you would like me to accompany you?'

'I should be very glad of your company, my dear fellow. Though it is a capital mistake to theorise without sufficient data, I confess a picture is beginning to form in my mind. And it is a far from pleasant one.' Holmes stared out through the rain-splattered window as the omnibus began to pick up speed along the Haymarket. 'There is nefarious business afoot, Watson. Two men have been brutally slain and, unless we can get to the bottom of the affair, I have no doubts that others will follow.'

* * *

After leaving the omnibus at the corner of Baker Street, Holmes called in at the telegraph office while I continued on to our lodgings. Mrs. Hudson informed me, to my delight, that my meat and potato pudding had been kept in a warm oven and it was back on the table in front of me before Holmes had returned. He duly went straight to his room, reappearing ten minutes later as the scruffiest vagabond I had ever clapped eyes on. He carried with him a battered frock-coat, a pair of trousers torn down one leg and a woollen hat. I knew instantly who they were intended for.

'Holmes, really!'

'If you wish to accompany me, I'm afraid I must insist,' he replied. 'You will not blend in around the docks looking like that.'

I conceded the point and, after finishing my dinner, went up to my room to change. I found the business of assuming such a disguise to be rather enjoyable and, for extra effect, adopted a limping gait that had been a common feature of my life for several months after returning from Afghanistan.* When I shuffled back into the sitting room, Holmes congratulated me and pointed towards a dish of wet dirt on the table.

'A liberal application on the hands and perhaps a daub on two on the face,' he said, 'then we can be off. Mrs. Hudson has sent for a cab.'

The waiting cabby was alarmed to see two such shabby men leave a respectable address and insisted on the full fare in advance before taking us anywhere. We were dropped off just prior to reaching the streets around Victoria Dock and walked the rest of the way.

It was now past nine o'clock but the area remained a hive of activity. The tall masts of the docked ships could be seen over the roofs of the warehouses that lined the river and there was a constant stream of traffic driving back and forth along the Victoria Dock Road.

'Where do we start?' I asked.

'The public houses around here are a hot-bed of local gossip,' said Holmes. 'We can just take our pick. Let me do the talking though, my dear fellow. If these people think they're being interrogated, they'll give you nothing but a thick 'un for your trouble.'

We chose a tavern on the corner of Nelson Street, a run-down thoroughfare located about halfway between Roscoe

Street, where the vagrant had pawned Carletti's possessions, and the main entrance to the wharves by Bugsby's Reach. Ordering two pints of their best beer, the taste giving me cause to wonder what on earth their worse must be like, we sat at a table in the corner. Holmes made conversational pleasantries with the dock-workers sitting at the next table and, with me marvelling at the ease with which Holmes manipulated the chat, slowly got them to divulge all they knew about the vagrant who had been arrested for the local murder. Holmes's gentle coaxing, making it appear the dockers were providing the information off their own backs, was very clever and we soon had the information we needed. The vagrant's name was Charles Adams, a former Light Infantryman. Upon his release from custody that afternoon, Adams had paid the rounds of the local public houses, relating the circumstances of his absence to anyone who would listen, none of whom probably knew he was missing in the first place.

'Ah, Adams, of course!' Holmes had

said just before we left the pub. 'He's that old soak who's a permanent fixture by the war memorial.'

'No, mate, you're wrong,' one of the dockers had replied. 'His patch is over by the slips.'

'Yes, indeed,' Holmes said. 'My mistake.'

We made for the slips straightaway and, true enough, found Charles Adams holding court around a flaming brazier, regaling others of his ilk with the tale of his time in the cells at Poplar police station.

'Let me go, they did,' the grizzled old campaigner was heard to say, 'just like that. Not so much as a bye or leave, just opened the door and told me to clear off, they did.'

'It won't do to discuss matters openly,' Holmes said as we observed the gathering. 'I shall have to get Adams alone. Here's some money, Watson. Pop into that store over there and buy a couple of bottles of their cheapest liquor.'

I did as I was asked and returned to find Holmes warming his hands around the brazier.

'Ah, my dear friend Pagnell!' he cried in a thick Irish brogue. 'What did I tell you, lads? Finest dipper in the city an' no mistake! Who fancies joining us in a drink?'

Within minutes, Holmes had struck up a conversation with Adams and, while I kept the others plied with alcohol, they slipped away to the river wall. Out of the corner of my eye, I watched Holmes question the vagrant. At first he seemed to protest before finally yielding and talking freely. Eventually, Holmes pressed some money into Adam's hand and nodded for me to join him.

'I simply asked straight out where he got the Italian's possessions and offered him a choice of suitable remuneration for a truthful account or swift retribution if he kept silent,' Holmes told me as we walked along the path by the river wall. 'It cost me a pretty penny or two, Watson, but it was worth it. Late on Wednesday night, Adams was approached by a jarvey who said he had a deal going with a wharfinger to smuggle out some goods from the

docks; porcelain figures, he was told.*
Would Adams like to earn himself a few
bob and keep watch while they nip in
and bring it out? He said he would and
was paid fifteen shillings for his trouble,
hoping it would become a regular billet.

'All went well but, as the growler was
leaving the docks, the jarvey tossed a
paper bag down to Adams as they passed.
'A bonus!' he called out. The bag
contained a gold neck-chain, a pocket-
watch and an empty leather wallet.'

'Why should they do such a thing?' I
asked. 'They could have just disposed of
Carletti's possessions in the Thames when
they dumped the body?'

'They were far cleverer than that,
Watson,' said Holmes. 'The murderers
knew the vagrant would pawn the items
locally and, should the body ever be
traced back to Victoria Dock, which
would have been unlikely had it not got
snagged, he would be putting himself in
the frame for Carletti's murder. Think of
it as a contingency plan and a deucedly
clever one at that.'

'But if they hoped Adams would take

the blame, why did they commit a second murder in an identical fashion? It only served to prove the vagrant's innocence and reopen the investigation.'

'I must admit, you have me there,' conceded Holmes. 'All they had to do was wait for Adams to swing and they could have continued their murderous spree unfettered. Such an action can only suggest the second murder *had* to take place when it did.'

'*Had* to?'

'That is the only conclusion that can be reasonably drawn.'

We walked along the pathway for several more minutes before turning away from the river and heading through a warren of narrow streets back into Victoria Dock Road. Holmes, having visited the area twice before and, if I knew him, having studied his detailed city maps before setting out, led us directly to a cab-yard where, after once again being obliged to settle the fee in advance, secured transportation home.

'Back to Baker Street, Holmes?'

'Yes, there is nothing more to keep us

here. Tomorrow will bring further avenues of inquiry. I am expecting a reply to my wire and there is also the curious matter of the ring.'

'The ring?'

'Carletti's wedding band, Watson. The paper bag tossed from the growler contained only his wallet, his pocket-watch and a gold neck-chain. Adams swears on his life there wasn't a ring and I believe him. It was not on Carletti's person, nor was it in his hotel room for I searched it thoroughly. It is suggestive, is it not?'

'What can it mean?'

We settled back into the cab as it moved out of the yard and along the main thoroughfare.

'I shall have to consider the matter in the time honoured fashion, my dear fellow,' Holmes said. 'A comfortable chair, a roaring fire and a pipe or two of my favourite blend. I can think of nothing more conducive to the thought process. I would also add that an hour with my Stradivarius may help but you look dead to the world, my dear Watson, and I cannot help but fear you would be tempted to break the instrument over my head if I prevented you from having a good night's sleep!'

5

I was greeted at the breakfast table the next morning by Sherlock Holmes waving a piece of paper above his head.

'A reply from Toller!' he announced triumphantly. 'They have identified the second victim!'

He handed me the yellow telegram slip, which I proceeded to read aloud. ''Arthur Warren, solicitor, 31, resides with parents at 'The Maples', East Acton. Reported missing yesterday morning after failing to return home. Jones now in charge. Toller.''

'Do you still play billiards at your club with that barrister fellow?' Holmes asked as I joined him at the table.

'Thurston? Yes, as often as I can,' I replied. 'I've come on enormously over the past few months. The trophy may very well have my name on it this year.'

'Might I suggest you call on him this morning? He may have heard of this

Warren and perhaps knows where he was based. It will save time going through the official channels for I can find no mention of him in the directories.'

'Certainly,' said I, pouring myself a cup of tea. 'And what will you be doing today?'

'I have a theory as to the location of the missing ring, Watson, and, like all theories, it needs to be put to the test. If I am correct in my thinking, I will have that very ring here on the table by this afternoon.

'And just how, pray, will you manage to do that?'

'A letter of authority from Whitehall, a shilling or two of shoe leather and an irate bank manager,' smiled Holmes. 'That will be all.'

★   ★   ★

I visited Clive Thurston at his Brompton home and, over a delicious roast beef lunch with him and his good lady wife, for which they insisted I join them, I discovered he knew Arthur Warren personally. He was devastated when I broke the news of his death. Warren's billet was at Harcourt & Boswell, a small firm of solicitors specialising in building leases. I returned home with a wealth of information, not to mention a full stomach, and waited over two hours for Holmes to do likewise.

'Have you been as successful as I?' I enquired as my friend entered the sitting room.

'Ah! You have traced Warren's place of work, I take it?'

'Number 24 Praed Street, 3rd floor. Thurston knew him personally. A decent chap by all accounts, a little quiet but with no vice in him. It seems he had a highly promising future.'

'Capital, Watson! I shall call there first thing tomorrow.'

'And what about you? How was your day?'

Holmes reached into his pocket and flicked what I thought was a sovereign across the room. It was not until I had caught it that I realised it was, in fact, a gold wedding band.

'Holmes!' I cried out in astonishment. 'Where on earth did you find it?'

'I've been slow off the mark in this case, Watson. Decidedly slow.' Holmes poured himself a drink and sat down opposite me. 'Consider the facts. A man is in the country on a secret assignment for his government. He makes his own travel arrangements and uses a pseudonym. It would be foolish, would it not, after going to such lengths to maintain the secrecy, to take highly confidential and sensitive papers back to his hotel room? Now, Carletti left the Whitehall Mansions at just before five and was seen arriving back at Buxton's, all of a mile away, at half past the hour. What does that suggest to you?'

'That he stopped off somewhere?'

'Precisely. There are a fair number of banks along that stretch and I wired the manager of each of them with my inquiry and note of my governmental authority. I received a reply from the manager of the Brand & Co. Bank in Salisbury Street, just off the Strand, confirming a safety-deposit box had been opened in the name of Buffón on Monday, the day Carletti arrived in the city. The manager wasn't too happy about coming into the bank on a Sunday morning, I can tell you.'

'And he allowed you to look inside the box?'

'Not without a police warrant, Watson, but my letter of authority from Whitehall was enough to obtain one. I've no doubt Jones will get to hear of it but we shall deal with that small problem when the time comes. I opened the box in the presence of the bank manager and Sergeant Cox of E division to find it contained several documents pertaining to the naval treaty and *that*.'

Holmes gestured to the wedding ring I held in my hand.

'But why did he put it in the security box?'

'Consider Carletti's actions the night he disappeared, Watson. He told the hotel porter he was going to the theatre. I suggest that was a lie and that he intended to visit a rather different form of establishment for a rather less wholesome form of entertainment.'

It took me several moments to realise what Holmes was driving at, much to his amusement.

'Holmes, if what you are suggesting is true,' I responded, 'I hardly think it would matter whether he had a ring on his finger or not as long as he had enough money in his pocket.'

'But Carletti was a gentleman, Watson,' Holmes said, 'and a Catholic, though hardly a devout one, the gold neck-chain pawned by Adams had a crucifix charm. Committing adultery is one matter, doing it while wearing your wedding band, a beloved gift from your wife, and a symbol of your lasting unity in the eyes of the Lord, is another.'

'The cad.'

Holmes threw back his head and roared with laughter. 'For a man with experience of women in three continents, Watson, you can be remarkably pious at times.'

In spite of my annoyance at the remark, I elected not to add fuel to the fire by remonstrating. I lit my pipe and, after a few minutes of silence had restored the former atmosphere, asked: 'And do Carletti's private papers give you any clues?'

'They are all in Italian, my dear fellow, so I am at a loss to their exact contents, save the odd word or two. I do not believe they have a bearing on the case in any event.'

'What will you do with them?'

'They will be secure in my safe overnight. I shall send word to Whitehall in the morning to have them collected, then I shall go on to Praed Street. If Carletti did visit a house of ill repute the night he died, it's possible Arthur Warren did likewise. Thurston said he was a man of no vice but that may prove to be an erroneous assessment of the man's character. There is little point my visiting East Acton either for his parents will have no knowledge of their son's private affairs and I have no wish to listen to them weep on about what a son of virtue he was. No, the people with whom Warren worked may be able to tell me a little more about him.

'Now, I fancy a spot of something to

eat. I won't ask you to join me, Watson, as I observe from your belt being a notch or two further along since this morning that you ate a hearty lunch at Thurston's.'

★ ★ ★

Sherlock Holmes and I left Baker Street together the next morning just after eighty-thirty. I took a cab to Clerkenwell while he made for Praed Street, all of half a mile away, on foot. I had left a notice on the door of the surgery as I left on Saturday, stating that, the following week, consultations would begin at nine and cease at five daily. I no longer felt able to put in the crippling fourteen-hour days and remained thankful that my time as Templeton's locum had just five and a half days to run.

Most of the patients that queued for my attention that cold Monday morning were suffering from heavy colds, victims of the weekend's persistent rain and wind, but several had severe pneumonia, one of which was carried into my consulting room on a makeshift stretcher constructed from two wooden planks and a length of twine, and needed urgent hospitalisation. My lunch-break was spent in the office of the nearby St. Luke's Hospital, desperately pleading with the Matron for the patient to be admitted and, in the end, agreeing to pay for the cost of their care myself.

Early in the afternoon, just after arriving back to the surgery, I received a curious note from Holmes. Hand-delivered by one of the Irregulars*, it asked me to bring home thirty bottles of *McCoy's Health Tonic*. I closed the surgery at five as planned and returned to Baker Street, struggling under the weight of the box of medicine. As I entered the sitting room, I was alarmed to see a suitcase on the table.

'Are you going somewhere, Holmes?' I called out, hearing my friend moving about in his bedroom.

'No, you are,' said he.

'I beg your pardon?'

'You will be spending the night at Buxton's Private Hotel in the Strand, my dear fellow. Forgive me for packing for you but time is short.'

'May I ask why?'

'You may indeed,' Holmes replied as he entered the sitting room. 'Your name is Patrick Smith and you are a commercial traveller from Liverpool. You will find your business card upon the table. Ah, you have the tonic! Excellent! They are your samples, Watson, for what is a commercial traveller without his samples?'

'And just why is Patrick Smith from Liverpool staying at Buxton's Private Hotel?' I carefully placed the box of medicine on the table and looked into the suitcase. It contained several changes of clothes, a nightshirt and a leather toilet box, new to me, commemorating the '85 Aintree Grand National.

'I visited Arthur Warren's place of work but his superiors were unable to furnish me with any information of relevance,' Holmes explained. 'On the contrary, they considered him to be an admirable young chap and a devastating loss to the firm. Inspector James arrived just as I left but I managed to duck into a nearby doorway and he didn't see me. He came out ten minutes later practically smoking from the ears! I fear there may be repercussions there, Watson.'

'Anyway, I returned at lunchtime and approached a young solicitor who had the desk opposite Warren. I bought him lunch at the King's Arms and, after being assured what he told me would not go any further and his name not brought into the matter, he told me all he knew about Warren's private life. Apparently, every Friday evening, Warren visited an establishment somewhere in Chelsea, he didn't know exactly where, returning home to East Acton on the late train.'

'And what has this to do with my visiting Buxton's?'

'Gianluca Carletti was a stranger to the city and would hardly know the whereabouts of such places. He must have received his information from somewhere.'

'Someone at the hotel, you mean?'

Holmes sat down in the basket chair and prepared himself a pipe, lighting it with a burning ember from the fire. 'In my experience, Watson, a hotel porter has a far better knowledge of the illicit establishments in this city than the whole of the Metropolitan Police force. Whatever your fancy, be it opium, ratting, gambling, cock-fighting, prize-fighting or simply the company of a young lady, the hotel porter can service your every need. For the gentleman traveller, away from home and seeking excitement, he is always the first port of call.'

'Holmes, I do not like where this is leading.'

'When you check in at Buxton's, make sure you tip the porter handsomely. Tell him you may require a little local information after dinner, perhaps accompany it with a discreet wink, he will understand your meaning.'

The thought of carrying out such a task hardly filled me with confidence. Disguising myself as a vagrant to visit Victoria Dock was one thing — I hardly spoke and even then it was just a series of grunts. This was very different. Holmes was a marvellous actor, indeed he had been on the stage briefly as a young man, and possessed a wide range of characters and accents, each as fully authentic as the other. If ever he found himself in the same room as someone from Glasgow, Cornwall, the Welsh valleys or even further afield such as New York or even Johannesburg, Holmes would begin to talk in a like accent. Such a show would usually result in him being invited to dinner, questioned enthusiastically about his lineage and altogether treated as a long-lost friend. It was very rare that somebody reacted with suspicion. In fact, it only happened once to my knowledge, by a Professor of Languages from Chicago, and Holmes skilfully deflected the gentleman's doubt by remarkably answering each and every question that was put to him about the city's landmarks and heritage.

'Holmes, you would be better suited to this sort of thing than me,' I protested, pacing across the room.

'Nonsense, my dear fellow, I have complete faith in you. Besides, my face is already known at Buxton's for I spent some time there on Thursday afternoon, do not forget, questioning the staff and searching Carletti's room.'

I frowned in resignation and sat down at the table.

'Tell me what you want me to do,' I sighed.

★ ★ ★

The address in Chelsea where the porter assured me I would receive a warm welcome was in total darkness. There was no evidence anyone was even in the building, a three-storey dwelling similar to those in Baker Street, let alone it being a lively establishment for discerning gentlemen as promised. I stepped from the cab, pulled the collar of my coat up high around my neck to ward off the cold night air and handed payment to the cabby.

'It looks deserted,' I said. 'There's no sign of life anywhere.'

'Nor should there be,' said Sherlock Holmes. 'Discretion is the order here. Off you go, my dear fellow, and do not worry. I shall be close at hand.'

I took a deep breath and strode as confidently as I could across the quiet street. Behind me, I heard the hansom moving off and realised, despite Holmes's reassuring words, I was all alone. I knocked gingerly on the door with my cane and was startled to then see a pair of eyes staring out at me through a small panel set into the door.

'Oh, good evening to you,' I said. 'My name is Smith. I was told you may be able to help me?'

'Yeah?' came the vaguely threatening retort.

'Yes. Er, Chalky said I would be very welcome here.'

With that, the panel closed and, a moment or two later, the door swung silently open. I glanced to my side to see the hansom cab driven by my friend turn out of sight at the end of the street before stepping across the threshold.

Discretion, a sense of propriety and a lack of desire to trouble the reader unnecessarily prevents me from furnishing a complete description of the time I spent within those walls. The reception room into which I was shown, after being relieved of my hat, coat and cane, was a large and exquisitely furnished chamber with deep-pile carpeting, crystal chandeliers and, at the far end, a grand piano.

There were some twenty to thirty people in the room at a guess, gentlemen outnumbering the fairer sex by a good four or five to one, all dressed in their best evening attire and conversing in small groups. A crowd of around eight were gathered around the piano where a young man with shoulder-length hair was holding court, playing delightful ditties with humorous, although somewhat questionable, lyrics.

I bought an exorbitantly-priced drink from the bar, the information from the porter having already set me back half a guinea, and settled in a discreet corner of the room, supposedly to read one of the many newspapers and periodicals available but in reality to observe in some depth both the room and its singular inhabitants. There was a large, ornamental staircase close to where I sat and I watched with interest the light but constant traffic between the two floors.

Over the next hour, I was approached by at least half a dozen gentlemen and, during the numerous conversations that took place, was offered a place at a card table, stocks in a new South African mining concern, imported cigars from Cuba cheaper than any tobacco emporium in the city and the address of a gent in Limehouse selling the best fighting dogs mony can buy.

I politely refused all such offers but one I was subsequently made when returning to the bar for a further drink, a mere soda-water this time, presented me with more of a dilemma. I was approached by a young lady, striking in appearance courtesy of a vivid electric blue dress and a length of stunning red hair, who inquired in a gentle voice with the barest hint of a West country accent whether I would like to accompany her upstairs. Finding a way of seeing the upper floors of the building had been troubling me for some time but considered such a tactic, despite Holmes's apparently base opinion of my morals, to be the last I would resort to.

Finding her solicitation kindly declined, the young woman turned her attention to an elderly man sitting at the far end of the bar. He did not need a second invitation and the two of them made off, arm in arm, towards the stairs.

'Not your cup of tea, eh?'

I looked around, a little startled, to see a man taking a seat at the bar beside me.

'What? No, no, I was . . .'

'What's your vice, sir, if you don't mind me asking? Cards, perhaps?'

I recognised the man, aged in his late-forties and with a large and heavily waxed moustache, as one who had been involved in a card game in view from where I had been previously sitting. It was clearly played for very heavy stakes for I observed at least five pounds changing hands.

'Heavens, no,' I said. 'I'm afraid my finances could not take the strain.'

A plan was beginning to formulate in my mind. Holmes had shown the day before how clever questioning could be used to gain information and, following his example, I could learn all I needed to about the upper floors without visiting them. The gentleman seemed an ideal mark, his slight unsteadiness when taking his seat a sure sign of him having imbibed a little too much that evening.

'My name is Smith,' I said.

'Aren't they all?' he laughed.

I cursed Holmes for choosing such an obvious pseudonym and chuckled along to hide my embarrassment. I later discovered the choice of my identity was down to the only suitable business card Holmes happened to have at the time, one of a dozen he had pocketed for future use when visiting a New Cross dentist several months before.

'On this occasion, it happens to be true.' I offered my hand and it was shaken amiably. 'Patrick Smith.'

'Stephenson,' the man replied. 'Dr. Stephenson.'

'Ah, a medical man! I'm in health tonic myself. *McCoy's*, do you know of it? Marvellous stuff!'

'No, I can't say that I do, Mr. Smith,' said Stephenson. 'I am no longer in general practice. I have discovered a far more profitable venture than exposing myself daily to the myriad of illness and disease that permanently infests our population.'

I sensed another business opportunity was about to be put to me but managed to hold my expression of interest.

'Tell me, Mr. Smith, what does a man like yourself, being on the fringes of the established medical order, think of spiritualism?'

The question was like a bolt out of the blue and I struggled to maintain my countenance. The final thing Holmes had said to me before we left Baker Street was to join in all conversations with interest, particularly those concerning spiritualism or the supernatural, though ensuring I stayed non-committal on the subject at all times. He would elucidate no further on the matter and Stephenson's question had therefore seriously unnerved me.

'Well, I have to admit not to have given it much consideration, Dr. Stephenson,' I said. 'The people I deal with may throw their hands up at such talk but I think there could possibly be more to this world than meets the eye.'

Stephenson produced a monocle from his pocket and fixed it to his eye before continuing the conversation. 'And you are in health tonic, you say, Mr. Smith? Some kind of commercial traveller, I take it?'

'Yes, based in Liverpool. I am only in London for a day or two. This is my first time here, in fact.'

'How interesting,' he said. 'How very interesting, indeed. Here, let me get you another drink. No, no, I insist. Barman? Another whisky for my friend!'

★ ★ ★

As I stood on the pavement with Dr. Stephenson, cordially discussing the latest racing news, I prayed the hansom cab driven by Holmes would be the first to approach. To my horror, a four-wheeler came into view and, without any word or gesture from Stephenson, drew to a stop where we stood. My new-found companion opened the door and, stepping aside, invited me to board first.

'After you, Patrick.'

'Thank you.'

As I stepped into the carriage, with no sight of Holmes anywhere along the street, I swear my heart missed several beats. Stephenson got in beside me and we began to move off. The blinds on the windows were secured and I could hardly turn to gaze out of the small window in the back of the carriage without attracting comment. The invitation from Stephenson, during a discussion on seances and the afterlife, to leave the warmth of the Chelsea house and call upon a small social gathering of like friends had roused my suspicion to the point where, as dangerous as it may seem, I felt compelled to accept. I had not expected Stephenson to have a private carriage waiting. I just prayed that Holmes had seen us leave and, at this very moment, was dogging our progress through the London streets.

As the carriage began to gain speed, a thousand thoughts were competing for primary attention in my mind. Did Holmes suspect a spiritualist connection to Carletti and Warren's deaths? Were the mutilations on their bodies the mark of some sort of horrific ritual? Did Carletti and Warren ride in this very carriage to meet their murderous end? If the answer was yes, I knew my fate lay solely in the hands of Sherlock Holmes. Several times during the journey, during which Stephenson and I continued in conversation, I believed I could hear the noise of a hansom cab close behind. At other times, though, the streets appeared to be in silence. I had neglected to bring my Webley in case I was searched upon entering the house in Chelsea and my cane was the only weapon I had to hand.

Some forty minutes after setting off, I felt the carriage turn sharply to the left and head along a very narrow gravel track. The slenderness of it could be determined from the faint sound of tree branches and leaves scraping along both sides of the vehicle, a deduction I believed Holmes would be proud of.

The carriage finally stopped and Stephenson and I alighted. I found myself in the driveway of a large town house, set some distance back from the road and bordered on all sides by a range of tall cedar trees. As I followed Stephenson towards the front door, I glanced over my shoulder along the gravel track. There was no sign of any other vehicles or pedestrians on the road and the seriousness of my situation sunk in. I had taken matters into my own hands and, for all I knew, could now be about to walk in very real danger. Whatever lurked behind the door of this nondescript grey-brick town house, I would have to face it alone.

6

Over the nearly forty year period in which I have chronicled the adventures of my distinguished friend, I have never sought to adopt a standard formula of practice. Some cases were written up in my journal almost immediately, while the facts remained fresh, where others were not set down on paper for many years, often leading inadvertently to the odd error creeping into the published account, usually concerning dates. I am writing my account of this particular case some considerable time after it occurred, mainly due to the quite shattering effect it had upon my nerves. It has only been with the passing of time that I am at last able to revisit the events of that night in my mind.

* * *

There seemed to be no domestic staff on duty in the house and, after hanging our hats and coats on an already overfull stand in the hall, Dr. Stephenson and I made our way into a well-furnished though somewhat stuffy drawing room. The Doctor's friends were of a surprising mix; a former military man who had served in the Indian campaigns, a retired factory owner and his wife, a young gentleman of an excessively Bohemian nature and a woman of late middle-age who smoked a cigarette with the aid of an ivory holder.

I was greeted warmly by the assembled gathering and soon found myself sitting in a comfortable armchair with a whisky and a fine cigar, answering awkward questions about my life as a commercial traveller. I did not feel the interrogation was unwarranted, I was a stranger to them after all, or that they were suspicious of my bona fidés. Indeed, a bottle of '*McCoy's Health Tonic*' was soon produced from my inside pocket and passed around the gathering, admittedly with mixed reviews. It was Sherlock Holmes who had told me to keep a bottle of the medicine with me at all times.

'Commercial travellers are never off duty, my dear fellow,' he had said just before we left our lodgings that evening. 'I have been offered samples of imported cigarillos at a funeral, books of fabric squares in a concert hall and French postcards in the waiting room of Charing Cross Station. The latter proved an unfortunate incident as an attempt to apprehend the scoundrel left me without my left canine.'

Rather my feeling of awkwardness came from my own fear of saying something that would betray the truth, that I was not who I purported to be and had never been to Liverpool in my life. Fortunately for me, neither of the other guests claimed any knowledge of the city and I found myself able to regale tales of the Liverpool life without fear of contradiction. The conversation was not, I must add, entirely one sided. Indeed, I had actively sought to discover as much as I could about this strange gathering and asked as many questions as were put to me but the answers I received in reply proved of little value.

'Mr. Smith here has only just arrived in London,' Stephenson announced, topping my glass up with a further serving from the whisky decanter, 'and is quite without kith or kin in the city. Is that not correct, sir?'

'Indeed, it is,' said I, as truthful a response as if the question had been put to Dr. John H. Watson himself instead of Patrick Smith. 'There is the odd business acquaintance, of course, but while I may tolerate their company during working hours, they're not the kind of people with whom I would choose to socialise. Quite insufferable some of them, to be sure.'

'Then it is indeed fortunate you have met some like-minded souls, Mr. Smith,' smiled Captain Hughes, the army veteran.

'Like-minded souls?'

'I am afraid you have jumped the gun, my dear Captain,' Stephenson laughed. 'Patrick is firmly sitting on the fence when it comes to matters of an other worldly nature. Is that not the case?'

'Oh, yes,' I chuckled. 'It would have to take something quite substantial for me to believe in the existence of the spirit world.'

'Perhaps we can provide you with that proof.'

This was the first time the enigmatic lady with the cigarette holder had spoken. I freely admit to finding her a powerfully attractive personality and it was clear she was held in high regard among the others in the room, particularly the young Bohemian chap who seemed quite besotted. She was of an indeterminable age, perhaps early to mid-thirties at a guess, and her skin had a quite ghostly pallor to it that I wasn't sure was the result of nature or cosmetics.

'Yes? And how, pray, do you intend doing that?'

'We gather here once every few weeks to attempt communication with those who have passed through to the other side,' explained the only other female in the room, a Mrs. Jeremiah Bootle. 'Mabel here is renowned throughout the Kingdom for her ability to provide a bridge between our two worlds.'

'A séance, you mean?'

'You disapprove, Mr. Smith?'

'Not at all,' chuckled I. 'I once went to one years ago, back in my university days, and had a splendid evening's entertainment. If I hadn't been able to see the thin lengths of cotton used to make the curtains wobble and the figure clad from head to toe in black surreptitiously moving objects around the room, I would've been seriously unnerved, I can tell you.'

'I assure you, Patrick, you will find no chicanery here,' Stephenson said. 'The room in which we attempt communication is well lit at all times. Only fraudsters or mere amateurs perform such an act in a darkened room.'

'Well, in that case, I would very much like to take part. Wouldn't mind trying to contact my late Uncle Sherlock actually. The old duffer promised me a hundred in his will but there was never any sign of it.'

I must admit it was something of a brave move on my part to mention such a unique Christian name in general conversation but considered the gamble a worthwhile one. Although at that time, in early 1886, Holmes was not known to the wider public, he had made something of a name for himself in both police and criminal circles. From what I could gauge, however, no one in the room showed even the slightest sign of recognition.

'Then it is time we began,' said Mabel, stubbing out her cigarette and getting to her feet. The rest of the gathering duly followed and I likewise. There was a definite weakness in my legs as I stood and I had to pause momentarily, holding onto the back of the armchair for support, before I felt able to walk. I had, of course, drunk several generous helpings of whisky since being admitted to the house, as well as those I had downed earlier in the evening in Chelsea.

'And where are you staying during your visit to London, Mr. Smith?' asked the young Bohemian, who I only knew as Jack, as we filed out of the drawing room and along the hall.

'Just a little boarding house out near Wapping,' I replied, 'nothing too fancy but suitable for my humble requirements and even humbler pocket.'

Holmes had strictly forbidden me to mention Buxton's Private Hotel to anyone I met within the establishment at Chelsea in case it set those who were responsible for Carletti's death upon their guard. The police had been all over the hotel in the past few days and there was still a young Constable on the premises when I checked in. Dr. Stephenson had already asked me the same question earlier while we were in Chelsea and I made sure the young man received the same response.

'You will find it difficult to get a cab back there this late at night,' Jack said, 'and our own horses will have been stabled already. They've been on the go since first light, bless them. You really must stay here tonight and we can give you a lift back first thing tomorrow morning.'

'No, no, I couldn't possibly impo . . .'

'Nonsense, we insist,' said Stephenson, bringing up the rear of the party. 'Unless you will be missed?'

'Only the landlady knows I am in London,' I replied, cursing the effect the amount of alcohol I had drunk was having on my lower limbs, 'and she leaves the front door key under a flower pot. No doubt she is already well asleep by now.'

'Then the matter is settled. Ah, here we are. Be a good fellow, young Jack, and kindly assist Patrick down the stairs. It seems he is a little unsteady on his legs.'

★   ★   ★

I retain little knowledge of the precise chain of events over the next hour or so and, for that, I am truly grateful. I was assisted down a steep flight of steps into what was once a wine cellar but had been kitted out as a permanent venue for spiritualist activities. The walls were draped with finely woven tapestries, depicting, as far as I could tell in the low light, a variety of astrological patterns and symbols. The room was illuminated only by a small number of candles, all of which appeared to have been freshly lit only moments before we entered the room and, I guessed, probably the work of the carriage driver whom I had not seen or heard since alighting from the vehicle in the driveway. The centrepiece of the room was a low oval table, covered with a deep red cloth and surrounded by an array of floor cushions.

I was guided by Bohemian Jack to a plain wooden chair in the corner of the room, the only piece of such furniture in sight, and sat and watched impassively as the table was prepared for the séance. Both Jack and Jeremiah Bootle made small talk with me but, save for the odd grunt and nod, I was quite unable to reciprocate. The only way out of the basement was via the staircase and I did not relish my chances of reaching the top unchallenged should events cause me to make a run for it, especially as my legs felt as if they belonged to somebody else. I closed my eyes and offered a silent prayer. I have never been man to whom religion has come easy, even in spite of seeing on the battlefields of Afghanistan just how comforting the presence of the Padre was to a dying man. My prayers were not directed to the almighty but to someone who had earned my faith. Sherlock Holmes.

'It is time. Bring him forward.'

I felt myself being lifted out of the chair and taken across the room to the table. My legs had practically turned to jelly and my eyes were having trouble focusing. My mind, though, remained clear and it was racing. This was to be no ordinary séance.

'No, no . . . ' I heard myself mumble weakly. 'Have to go now. A . . . an appointment. Please, I . . . '

My pitiful pleas went unanswered and I was gently coerced into sitting down on one of the cushions at the side of the table. My head began to spin and I knew at that moment alcohol was not solely to blame for my condition. I had been fed some sort of sleeping draught, either in the whisky or perhaps even the cigar.

What followed was a bizarre ritual in which Mabel, shrouded in a gown as black as coal, held court; chanting what can only be described as a series of idolatries towards a small fetish, surrounded by an arrangement of candles in the shape of a five-pointed star, that had been placed in the middle of the table. The rest of the gathering, clad in similar robes which I confess I do not recall seeing them don, sat with their heads bowed and their eyes closed. Although the opportunity was presented, for the life of me, I was not able to get to my feet and effect an escape. Physically, I was all but paralysed and it remained the sole use of my collective energies just to keep myself from falling asleep.

The individual words of the mantra soon became indistinct to me, merging into one foul noise that reverberated around my head. All the strength I possessed at that point was no longer sufficient to combat the growing drowsiness and my eyes fell closed.

*   *   *

It was a sharp pain in the centre of my chest that caused my eyes to burst open once more. I found myself prostrate upon the table, the idol and the candles having been removed to a high shelf at the side of the room, with the five shrouded figures, the hoods pulled up over their heads, looming over me. I attempted to move but, though my body was not bound by any physical restraints of any kind, found I could not do so. I managed to lift my head slightly and saw to my horror a thin laceration running across my abdomen. I realised that was how both Gianluca Carletti and Arthur Warren had met their deaths; lured to this house by Dr. Stephenson after meeting him at the establishment in Chelsea and slain on this altar as part of some sickening, satanic ritual, and that I was destined to die the same. I felt warm hands upon my body and saw several of the shrouded figures, I know not which as their features were obscured in shadows, run their fingers through the stream of blood that ran down the side of my torso.

It was the figure to the immediate left of me that bore the weapon that had caused my wound. It was a plain surgical scalpel with a thin, almost delicate blade. I was utterly powerless as the knife was once more lowered ceremoniously to the midriff and a further cut drawn slowly through the skin. My mouth opened involuntarily, as if to let out a cry of pain and anguish, but I heard no sound emanate. My body and its functions were frozen but my reason was active. How I wished at that point to be struck dead where I lay than face further torture at the hands of such fiends.

For how long I lay upon that table, I do not know. I drifted in and out of consciousness and, to be candid, did not feel the additional incisions that were delicately carved upon my helpless body. I found myself cursing Sherlock Holmes and, strangely enough, myself for how I would be letting down the poor and needy of Clerkenwell.

* * *

'It is the moment.'

I forced myself to open my eyes and was greeted with a sight more terrifying than any I have ever encountered. Only coming face to face with the Giant Rat of Sumatra in the sewers beneath Millbank in the autumn of '95 came close and that is a story, due to the involvement of several people of noble standing, that may remain forever untold. The figure to my left was handed a polished wooden box, similar to an ornamental pistol case with brass fittings and a red velvet interior, from which a dagger was produced.

It measured some ten inches in length, including the finely decorated handle, and the narrow blade, sharpened to a point, glistened menacingly in the flickering candlelight. I recognised the type of weapon as a misericord, designed for performing the *coup de grâce*. How I yearned to scream out my true identity, how Holmes would stop at nothing to bring to justice those responsible for my death, to hunt them into their graves. My protestations were silent, however, and I knew further attempts to make myself heard, to plead desperately for my life, would be in vain.

'Hold his arms,' Stephenson's voice said and I knew it was to be the Doctor himself who was to render the final act. Strong hands, I guessed belonging to

Bohemian Jack, pinned me to the table to ensure I made no final gesture of defiance. I shuddered as Stephenson ran the tips of his fingers along the left front of my torso, searching for the precise point as which the blade would be inserted. I closed my eyes tightly and, if it were possible to wish oneself to death, I would willingly have taken my own life at that moment.

I took no notice of the number of dull thuds that began to echo around the cellar, my only thought that of damning the further suffering Stephenson seemed determined to inflict upon me by cruelly delaying the final blow. The hands clamping me to the table were suddenly relaxed but there was no resistance left in me, no reserves of energy or might that could be summoned in an instant to throw myself off the sacrificial altar.

'May God have mercy upon your souls!' cried a voice as I tensed myself for the end.

A hand was placed upon the centre of my chest and I felt warm breath upon my face.

'Watson!'

I opened my eyes to see Sherlock Holmes, the distress of a thousand men etched onto his face, looking down at me. I made to speak but, once again, found the words would not form in my mouth.

'Do not try to talk, my dear fellow. Help will be with you presently. After them, Inspector, after them!'

7

There are few sounds as comforting to me as those which perpetually filtered through the window of my second floor chamber at the rear of 221b Baker Street. The hustle and bustle of the busy thoroughfare, its intensity wholly dependant on the time of day, was a mere backdrop to the gentle blowing in the wind of the tall plane tree in the yard and the cheery family of birds that made their home among the branches. Many a time Holmes and I had returned to our lodgings at the conclusion of a case, each of us seeking a device by which a touch of normality could be restored to our lives. For my esteemed friend, it was some time alone with his Stradivarius or perhaps a pipe or two in front of the fire. For me, however, all could only be deemed right with the world when I lay safely in my bed.

I did not need to raise my eyelids to

realise I was in my own private chamber. The mixture of sounds so reassuringly familiar to me that I can even hear them now, some years after last setting foot across that particular threshold, at a time when the rhythmic glory of wheel and hoof has long since given way to the roar of the combustion engine. At first I remarked on the hellish nightmare it had been my misfortune to sleep through but a tightness across my chest as I gathered the sheets up to my neck, caused by a swathe of heavy bandaging, brought me swiftly back to reality. I threw back the covers and, the strapping severely restricting my range and speed of movement, donned my dressing gown and slippers. It was not a habit of mine to leave my bedroom without dressing first, a custom born from my military days, but I was anxious to see Holmes.

I made my way as fast as comfortably possible downstairs and into the lounge. Sherlock Holmes sat at the table, tucking into a plate of boiled potatoes and ham.

'Ah, my dear fellow! Awake at last!'

'What time is it?' I asked, glancing over

at the mantle clock.

'Past two in the afternoon. Tut, tut, man, do not concern yourself unnecessarily. Your patients are being taken care of.'

'Right. Well . . . that's good.'

I took my seat at the table and we sat in silence for what seemed an eternity. Sherlock Holmes suddenly bore the expression of a troubled, almost shamed, soul.

'Please accept my most profound apologies, Watson,' he said softly. 'I will never forgive myself for placing you in such a position. Never!'

'You saved my life, Holmes.'

'I very nearly ended it!'

Holmes leapt from his chair and strode across the room towards the window. He stood quite motionless, one hand resting his weight upon the frame, staring aimlessly out onto the busy street below. I poured myself a coffee from the fresh pot upon the table, allowing Holmes a moment or two to compose himself.

'Who was it who dressed my wounds? A professional enough job, I must say.'

'The duty police surgeon, a Doctor

McAuliffe, I believe. It is he, the poor soul, who is currently toiling away on your behalf in Clerkenwell.'

'I must write and thank him.'

'That will not be necessary, Watson. He is being paid a King's ransom.'

Holmes at last turned away from the window and returned to his seat. I quickly sought to assuage his feelings of guilt, mainly due to my own sense of culpability in the affair in so easily placing myself in the hands of such fiends.

'I really mustn't allow you to take full responsibility for what occurred last night,' I told him. 'It was completely foolish of me to leave the house with Dr. Stephenson the way I did. Completely inexcusable.'

'You did take me a little by surprise, I must admit,' Holmes said. 'I saw you both standing on the pavement from an upstairs window and, by the time I had got down to the street, you were very nearly out of sight. Fortunately, the cab was parked nearby.'

'You . . . you were in the building?'

'In a small room upon the second floor,

enjoying a rather pleasant, though expensive, conversation with a young lady. She picked me up at the bar after you politely gave her the brush off.'

I stared at Holmes in disbelief, completely lost for words.

'A white wig and beard, a pair of wire-framed glasses and a stoop to take six or so inches off my height,' he continued, 'can be extremely effective. I knew you had the situation downstairs commendably under control and was anxious to know what lurked on the floors above.'

'But why on earth did you keep your presence there from me?' I protested. 'Dash it all, Holmes!'

'Another matter in which I must crave your indulgence, my dear fellow. And the chap's name was Stephenson, eh? I must wire that small detail to Toller as soon as possible. It may prove quite invaluable.'

My fury at Holmes's lack of candour, not the last time in our long association he was to play such a trick★, was suddenly overshadowed by a far more foreboding thought as the ramifications of his last statement struck home.

'He is not in custody?'

'Alas, no.'

I decided the cup of coffee no longer possessed the restorative qualities I had required of it and instead made my way over to the whisky decanter. I poured myself a generous helping, considering it extremely well earned despite the early hour, and sat down in front of the small fire that was burning in the hearth.

'Perhaps you would like to start from the beginning?'

Leaving the remainder of his lunch untouched, Holmes joined me by the fire and lit himself a pipe. He took several long draws before pronouncing himself ready.

'I must confess I could not fathom any possible connection between the murders of Gianluca Carletti and Arthur Warren,' he began, 'except for the fact the same killer was clearly responsible. It was not until the reasons for the mutilations became clear to me that at last the jigsaw started to fall into place.'

'That both torsos were slashed to

conceal the signs of ritual sacrifice?'

'Indeed. I saw in the house in Hampstead, that is where you were taken by the way, a carving knife just fit for the purpose. No doubt it would soon have been put to work on you.'

I shuddered at the very thought of being brutalised in such a fashion and quickly took a soothing drink from the glass in my hand.

'The reason for you adopting the guise of Patrick Smith was simply to gain information regarding the whereabouts of the establishment visited by our two victims on the night they died and the means of gaining an entrance. It was certainly not to offer you up as the potential next victim, my dear fellow, I beg you to believe me on that point if nothing else.'

'I do, Holmes,' I reassured him.

'I had originally believed the murders took place in that very house in Chelsea. That is why I told you to join in any conversations of a spiritualist nature. Quite an erroneous deduction on my part. Your sudden departure for pastures new caught me completely unawares. I was very grateful for having the hansom, for it was only intended as somewhere I could change into my new persona without being seen.'

'And you followed me all the way?'

'I tracked your progress across the city as best I could but I eventually lost you somewhere in the vicinity of the Finchley Road. The carriage in which you were travelling had evidently turned off into a residential street but I was at a loss to know which. I was deeply tormented at the prospect of sending you to your death, Watson. I quickly summoned the help of a number of urchins playing nearby and, for a shilling apiece and the promise of half-a-guinea to the winner, they begun a systematic search of the neighbouring roads, looking for any signs that a four-wheeler had passed through there in the minutes before. They were not my usual Irregulars, Watson, but they displayed all the resourcefulness of that august association.

'I sent message to Inspector Toller through another of the lads and, in the meantime, followed up the leads with which the urchins had soon furnished me. Several driveways bore fresh carriage tracks and I discreetly checked each house in turn. I soon struck gold, Watson, in the form of your walking stick!'

I chuckled with delight at the remark but was forced to bring a halt to my outpouring almost immediately by the sharp pain it caused me in my lower abdomen.

'A stick, unmistakably yours, resting against the wall at the side of the front door,' Holmes resumed, 'clearly left to convey a message to me.'

'It was all I could think of doing,' said I. 'It was indeed fortunate that Dr. Stephenson stepped into the hall ahead of me.'

'You behaved splendidly, Watson. I conducted a quick reconnaissance of the property and its grounds and, when Toller and his men arrived, effected an immediate entrance. The jarvey was apprehended in the stables at the back of the house as he was preparing the growler that would have taken your body to its dumping ground. It may interest you to know that the sacks of feed in the stables were purchased from Greaves & Son, a local coster supplied by one Josiah Rumney.'

As much as I was pleased to hear Holmes's account of the night before, I still required an explanation as to the most disturbing aspect of all.

'And now perhaps you would care to clarify just how those devils who were upon the very verge of slaying me managed to escape custody?' I asked. 'There was only one way out of that cellar and they cannot have just vanished into thin air!'

'I am afraid you are quite wrong in that observation, Watson. There was a second door, located behind one of the tapestries that hung upon the wall. They all bolted through it the moment we forced our way in. The old couple did not get far, their advanced years not ideal for outrunning the long arm of the law, but the others were able to make their way into a thick copse that ran along the rear of the street. I set my new franchise of Irregulars onto them but, despite their nimbleness of foot and wide knowledge of the area, they were unable to pick up their trail. Have no fear, my dear fellow, they will not evade justice forever.'

'Perhaps Mr. and Mrs. Bootle will talk?'

'The elderly couple? They have remained tight-lipped so far,' Holmes said, reaching across to the fire and tapping out the remains of his pipe into the grate. 'Remind me not to purchase any more of Bradley's new Moroccan blend, Watson. It is far too bitter for my taste.'

'And have you determined a motive for the killings,' I enquired, 'and, more importantly, their timings? If I recall, you were convinced Warren's death *had* to occur when it did, even if it suggested to the police that the man they held for Carletti's death had to be innocent.'

Without a word, Holmes stood and walked over to his bureau. There upon the desk top, where I had failed to notice it before now, was a small object wrapped in what appeared to be a cotton shawl. He brought it back to the fire and handed it to me. I peeled back the covering with curiosity to be greeted by the sight of the strange fetish that had been the subject of worship before I took centre stage upon the altar.

'It is ghastly, Holmes!' I cried, turning my eyes away from the grotesque little figure. 'What on earth possessed you to bring it back here?'

'A souvenir, my good man, a souvenir! I already have a collection of relics from the criminal world that would put the Black Museum to shame!'

'And what is it exactly?'

'It appears to be African in origin, carved out of red mahogany and many hundreds of years old, but I am not sufficiently knowledgeable in the subject to comment further. I will seek out an expert in the next day or two and allow him to give me its provenance.'

'It has some spiritualist connection, obviously.'

'Oh, we are talking more than mere spiritualism, Watson. We have set foot in a world far darker than that of eccentric old ladies offering to make contact with the dearly departed.' Holmes paused before delivering the final, shocking denouement. 'Black magic.'

I physically shivered and reached for the poker to stoke up the fire, which was on the verge of burning out. 'And the timing of the murders?'

'The astrological charts on the wall tapestries may prove the key to unlocking that particular mystery, Watson. No doubt it will be shown that the sacrifices were made when and according to the constellation of the stars.'

My friend got to his feet once more and moved to the table where he swilled his mouth out with coffee, depositing the residual back into the pot. 'Moroccan! Huh!'

'And what happens now?' I asked. 'I hardly feel up to making a statement in my present condition but it must, of course, be done while the details are fresh.'

'Remain in your seat, my dear fellow,' replied Holmes. 'I think I can safely say you will not be troubled by the authorities any further.'

'What do you mean? Surely there must be some sort of inquiry?'

'What I mean, Watson, is that it is not in the best interests of the Italian or British Governments for this affair to reach open court. Gianluca Carletti's cover story was competent enough to book into a hotel room but will hardly stand up to thorough examination. As for young Warren, it may be the kindest thing to do to prevent the precise details of how he met his end from reaching the ears of his loved ones.'

'But these fiends mustn't be allowed to get away with murder, Holmes!'

'The old couple will be locked away in an asylum,' he said, 'far from the public gaze. As far as Carletti's pay-masters and Warren's family are concerned, the two slayings were committed by a deranged individual who is now under lock and key after confessing to the crimes. No trial, no investigation, no scandal.'

'And should the others be caught?'

'They will suffer the same fate. Whitehall will never allow a word of this to get into the press for fear of the secret treaty with the Italians becoming known. One day, it may be possible for the true story to be told.'

The thought of allowing the true nature of the crimes to remain a closely-guarded secret to all but a trusted few was abhorrent to me but, on further consideration, I was compelled to agree such a course of action was for the best. I did not relish my traumatic experience in that house in Hampstead becoming public knowledge and it is only now, after so many of those involved in the case have passed from the public conscious, that I feel warranted in setting matters right. This chronicle will be placed, with many others of a highly confidential or classified nature, or simply those where Holmes felt discretion was the order, in my old Army despatch box and placed in the care of the Charing Cross branch of the Cox & Co. bank. One day, long after I have gone to my final resting place, will the seal be broken and the nation privy to the facts.

★　★　★

I spent the next three or four days recuperating from my injuries, lavishly waited on by Mrs. Hudson. The lacerations I had suffered, eight in total and each made in relation to the others to form what Holmes considered to be an occult symbol, had not needed stitching and, with a regular change of dressing and application of a curative lotion, they soon healed. The emotional scarring remains to this day. I had given up all hope when lying upon that altar and the damage to my spirit was considerable. It was some time before I was able to sleep soundly at night and my nerves had been shot to pieces, a plight I can only compare to the low state of morale I found myself in after the Battle of Maiwand. It was my meeting with Sherlock Holmes and our subsequent involvement in the Jefferson Hope affair that caused my natural vivacity for life to begin to be restored. Once again, it was Sherlock Holmes who came to my rescue.

'A week enjoying the splendid air of the Peak country, Watson!' he announced, throwing open my bedroom door on the morning of Monday the 23rd. 'There is a train leaving St. Pancras at eleven and it is my intention we should both be on it. God speed now!'

I was thrilled at the chance to get out of London for a while and was soon packed and ready. We partook of an early lunch and, within just over an hour of my rising, were seated in a first class compartment of a train of the Midland Railway Company. It was most unlike Holmes to suggest such a trip and I questioned him on that point as the train pulled out of the station.

'You had a visitor early this morning, Watson, but I felt it best not to awaken you at such an hour in your present condition,' Holmes said. 'Young Templeton. It seems his sojourn in the bracing air of the Hallemshire hills has been of enormous value. They stayed at a small cottage in splendid isolation, some five miles from the nearest town, where the only call upon their time was fishing, rambling or watching the wildlife. As I have nothing on at present, I feel taking such a break ourselves will prove equally beneficial to both of us so I wired to see if the property was available. I do not mind admitting to you, my dear fellow, that this affair has taken its toll on me also.'

'Oh?'

Holmes took several moments to reply to my query, as if going over the horrific events of the past week in his mind. He lit himself a cigarette, his pipe and tobacco being stowed in the valise above his head, and gazed mournfully out of the window.

'Evil can manifest itself in an infinite number of ways, Watson. Who would have guessed that, behind the respectable façade of a Hampstead villa, a dark and dangerous game was afoot. And do not believe such things are the work of a maniacal few. London is a sewer, Watson, where the disease of depravity spreads and the battle, for those like myself who have dedicated their lives to the fight against crime, becomes more one of containment than conquest.

'I have never been a fellow for the open countryside, as well you know, but I confess at this moment to harbouring deep feelings of aversion for this great city of ours.'

I too turned my gaze upon the world beyond the window as the train gathered pace through the borough of St. Pancras. It was a grey, overcast day and heavy raindrops began to pepper the glass.

'We shall return to London refreshed in body and mind, Watson,' Holmes decreed with a smile. 'Ready for the next knock upon the door that may come our way.'

Postscript

There remain one or two issues surrounding the Carletti affair, as Holmes and I grew to refer to the case, that may be of interest to the reader. The secret naval treaty between Great Britain and Italy did indeed come to fruition after many months of confidential talks between the two nations. In fact, coincidentally, it became the focus of a further investigation a year later when the final draft of the treaty was stolen from the desk of an old school friend of mine employed at the Foreign Office. Sherlock Holmes was able to lay his hands on both the thief and the document without too much trouble and readers may find my chronicle of this case under the title of *The Naval Treaty*. I must state at this point that, owing to the need to protect the identities of several people involved with the case, it fell upon me to disguise several parts of the tale and set it in the summer of 1889, the year after my first marriage. I am now in a position to set the record straight and disclose that the theft of the document actually occurred in July 1887.

The location of the house of ill repute in Chelsea where Dr. Stephenson procured his victims was soon brought to the attention of the local police and plans set in motion to shut it down. Both Holmes and I felt this was a futile exercise, as those who frequented the club would simply take their particular vices elsewhere, and it was successfully argued that it was better to allow the house to remain open and a discreet eye kept on proceedings. There was no evidence to suggest the proprietors knew of Stephenson's activities and whatever else may have gone on under that roof, and however distasteful I may have felt it to be, it was no doubt one of many such establishments in our heaving metropolis and its very existence perhaps an inevitable one.

Despite the best efforts of Sherlock Holmes and Inspector Toller, who had been taken fully into our confidence, neither Bohemian Jack, Mabel or Captain Hughes were ever brought to justice. In fact, it was to be some years later before Dr. Stephenson finally received his due punishment for the murders of Gianluca Carletti and Arthur Warren. Changing his name and circle of friends to avoid detection, Stephenson continued to play an active role in the occult world, even lecturing on the subject and contributing to several pseudo-scientific journals. Using the pseudonym of Dr. Roslyn D Onston, he wrote many letters to London newspapers at the height of the notorious Whitechapel Ripper murders in 1888, theorising as to the identity and motives of the perpetrator, and was, I am now led to believe, even arrested and questioned on two occasions himself. It was not until 1904 that it was brought to my attention, by the then Chief Inspector Toller, that Dr. D Onston and Dr. Stephenson were one and the same. In spite of his apparent conversion to Christianity in 1893 and a record of good character since, there was no chance of allowing him to retain his liberty and Holmes himself returned from self-imposed exile on the Sussex Downs to oversee his arrest and incarceration in an asylum in Bedfordshire. The date of his death is not known.

Further research conducted by Toller in the weeks following this event suggests that the medium may have been one Mabel Collins, a noted spiritualist and Stephenson's former mistress. I was unable to make a positive identification after so many years, however, and no further action was taken.

There is one final matter left for me to bring to the attention of the reader regarding Dr. Stephenson. Although married at the time of the Carletti affair, his wife disappeared in May 1887 and was never seen again. Six portions of a woman's body were recovered from the Thames two days later. The remains showed signs of ritual mutilation.

★　★　★

Sherlock Holmes and I returned completely invigorated from our holiday in the Peaks, just as well for there was considerable call on my friend's services over the rest of the year. It proved to be his busiest period to date with such investigations as *The Beryl Coronet, The Mystery of Arnsworth Castle, The Darlington Substitution Scandal, The Case of Vittoria, The Circus Belle* and *The Tankerville Club Affair*. One of these cases is already a matter of public record while full details of the others have been placed, with this chronicle, in my despatch box, ready to thrill the world another day.

Notes

Chapter One

Holmes was wrong. Watson did indeed make a fine GP, running successful surgeries in Paddington (1888-90), Kensington (1890-94) and Queen Anne Street (1903-14) before rejoining his old Army regiment after the outbreak of the Great War.

Holmes eventually ceded to Watson's wishes the following year. A detailed narrative of the Hope case was published under the title of *A Study in Scarlet* at Christmas 1987.

Watson's brother, whose name we do not know, died in the late summer in 1888, just prior to *The Sign of Four* case.

Chapter Two

Although standard Army issue revolvers at the time were .450 Adams, this is the first occasion where Watson states his trusted weapon was, in fact, a Webley by manufacture. In the case of *The Adventure of the Speckled Band*, which occurred in April 1883, Holmes refers to Watson's 'Eley No. 2'. Webley No. 2 revolvers used Eley cartridges.

Chapter Three

Athelney Jones was later involved in Holmes's investigations into the Bishopsgate jewel robbery, a case Watson did not publish, and the murder of Bartholomew Sholto (see *The Sign of Four* case) while assigned to the City Police and 'R' division respectively. Inspector Peter Jones, who assisted Holmes in the case of *The Red-Headed League* is believed to be a horse of a different colour, despite seemingly possessing some knowledge of the Sholto case.

Chapter Four

Watson was injured in the Battle of Maiwand on July 27th 1880 where he was serving as a field surgeon with the Berkshires. Although the precise nature of his injuries are unclear, it appears he suffered bullet wounds in the shoulder, which shattered his collar-bone and grazed the sub-clavian artery, and his leg, damaging his achilles tendon.

jarvey — the driver of a cab or carriage
wharfinger — the manager of a wharf

Chapter Five

The Baker Street Irregulars; a group of street children recruited by Holmes to assist him in his investigations. Led by the redoubtable Wiggins, their first recorded appearance was in the Jefferson Hope case in 1881 (see *A Study in Scarlet*) but they had clearly been of valuable use before this.

Chapter Seven

The most notable occasion occurred during the celebrated case of *The Hound of the Baskervilles*. Holmes led Watson to believe he was in London when he was, in fact, encamped on the moor close to Baskerville Hall.

We do hope that you have enjoyed reading this large print book.

Did you know that all of our titles are available for purchase?

We publish a wide range of high quality large print books including:
Romances, Mysteries, Classics
General Fiction
Non Fiction and Westerns

Special interest titles available in large print are:
The Little Oxford Dictionary
Music Book, Song Book
Hymn Book, Service Book

Also available from us courtesy of Oxford University Press:
Young Readers' Dictionary
(large print edition)
Young Readers' Thesaurus
(large print edition)

For further information or a free brochure, please contact us at:
Ulverscroft Large Print Books Ltd.,
The Green, Bradgate Road, Anstey,
Leicester, LE7 7FU, England.
Tel: (00 44) **0116 236 4325**
Fax: (00 44) **0116 234 0205**